Until He Reigns

A DARK MAFIA ROMANCE

ARGENTIERI CRIME FAMILY
BOOK ZERO

JADA DARK

Copyright © 2023 by Jada Dark

All rights reserved.

No part of this book may be reproduced in any form or by any electronic or mechanical means, including information storage and retrieval systems, without written permission from the author, except for the use of brief quotations in a book review.

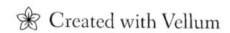

❀ Created with Vellum

Book Summary
UNTIL HE REIGNS (ARGENTIERI CRIME FAMILY)

Dante Argentieri is going to take everything from me.

My freedom. My happiness.

My innocence.

Why?

I deserve it.

I killed his father in cold blood. *I'm not sorry.*

Dante's coming for me. For vengeance. For my life.

He's going to make me do whatever he commands.

I get close enough to him to see the real pain inside his heart of steel.

He's just as broken as I am.

His illegal addiction to underworld crime rings won't be his downfall.

But his infatuation for me will be.

Until He Reigns is steamy, gritty, action-packed enemies-to-lovers, mafia romance featuring a mafia princes and a ruthless mob boss who's not seeking redemption.

Intended for mature readers only.

Author's Note

Dear reader!

Hi, it's Jada!

I appreciate you so much for choosing this book. Enjoy; but please be warned that this is dark mafia romance and some content may trigger sensitive readers.

Intended for mature readers only.

Playlist

Bubblegum Bitch - MARINA

Wolf in Sheep's Clothing - Set It Off

The Drug In Me Is You - Falling in Reverse

Sarcasm - Get Scared

Pass The Nirvana - Pierce The Veil

Animal I Have Become - Three Days Grace

Hayloft II - Mother Mother

One

Dante

I'm surrounded by people who claim to be loyal to me. Underbosses, maids, servants, bodyguards, sellouts, snitches, and women. So many damn people, and yet I feel so alone. They all come to me with their problems, expecting me to have the answers. But sometimes I just want to be left alone.

As I watch the stripper and dancer on stage, my mind wanders. Revenge is always on my mind, but sometimes I wonder if it's really worth it. All the sweat. Tears. All the pain. I helped build this empire, but what have I truly gained? Money, power, respect? It all seems so hollow.

The stripper who's been gifted to me for the night saunters over, kneels to the floor and grabs my belt. I catch her hand swiftly before she can proceed.

"Ask first," I bite out.

"Please..." She bats her long fake eyelashes and asks, "May I suck your cock?"

I lean back as she proceeds to suck my dick.

"Oh my...you are *well endowed*," she purrs.

I bite my lip and hold back a groan at the suction of her mouth on my shaft. Her lips and tongue glide up and down along its length until it is wet from her. She flicks her clit with her fingers as I throat pound her. I grab her hair in my fists and begin to ram my dick down her throat as she chokes, drooling on it with lust. The heat of her mouth makes me fuck her throat harder, faster. When it's all over her mouth is flooded with my cum, drooling down her chin.

She stands up as if she's about to sit on it, but I fold it back into my pants and zip up my fly.

"Oh come on," she purrs. "Can't we fuck?"

"No." She was just a means to an end of backed up tension filling up inside. She had served her purpose.

"Oh, why not? I'll be discreet."

She reaches out and tries to touch my face but I move it aside. "Leave."

She grumbles, and with her pussy clearly wet, she sashays in front of me.

"Now," I ordered.

She pouts as she walks away. I don't care. I have bigger things to worry about.

As I prepare another drink, Vito walks in and sits down. Vito Barbari is my right hand man, extremely loyal. Ever since my father handed me my first gun and started officially training me to take over for him in the event of his demise, Vito had been by my side. He used to be like an overbearing watchful protective uncle, but now he respects my decisions more. Not just because he has to, but because he knows I've come into my own. My father's demise came at a time when we least expected it, but that can be said about any man.

I hand Vito a drink.

"Did you fuck that bitch?" Vito asks as he sits down in the empty leather chair beside me.

"What the fuck do you think?" I reply.

"You know, Dante, you've been bringing too much attention to yourself. I know you think this club might be a good investment but I feel it has too many connections to that chump politician who tried to rig his election. You don't want your money tracked to him," Vito says.

"My money can't be tracked."

Vito takes a shot then leans forward. "Still, the place is falling apart at the seams. Owner needs to cut his losses. You shouldn't help him."

He is right, but I already know this.

"There's talk among the families," Vito continues. "You're bringing too much attention to yourself. As a young Mafia King, you need to remain in the shadows...always. You shouldn't get too popular with the politicians."

I scoff. "The families can fuck off. As long as I sit the head, I'll do what I want."

Vito shoots me a stern look. "If you want to keep your high standing, especially with that attitude of yours, you'd best find yourself a wife and fuck her until she bears your son. You've been at this four years already. It's time."

"Is this you talking or the families steering you off the deep end?" I ask.

"It's already written, Dante. There is a woman..."

I roll my eyes. "You mean the woman my father intended for me to marry?"

"Yes."

"Binetti is quite thirsty, isn't he? Well you tell Binetti I don't accept used goods."

Vito exhales harshly and leans back, squeezing the bridge of his nose. "So you will renege on that deal too? You're going to get yourself more enemies, Dante. The list is already lengthy."

I shrug. "Add his name to the top if you'd like. I don't give a damn."

But deep down, I know he's right. I need to start thinking about the future, about my legacy. I can't keep living like this. But the thought of settling down with someone I don't love, someone who was chosen for me, makes my skin crawl.

Someone knocks on the door and asks for Vito. He excuses himself and leaves. I drown myself in another stiff drink, staring out at the private show of strippers. I feel nothing as I watch them twirl and glide up and down poles and across the stage. The burn of the alcohol feels good as I take a sip, but it doesn't numb the pain inside. I need something more, something real.

I think about all the women I've been with over the years. They were all beautiful, all willing to do whatever I wanted. But they were all the same, in the end. They didn't truly know me, didn't truly care for me. They were just another way for me to pass the time.

I finish my drink and stand up, feeling restless. I need to clear my head. I stop at a street corner and look up at the stars. They're beautiful, but they don't mean anything to me. Nothing does, really. I'm just a man with too much power, too much money, and too little happiness.

But maybe that's just the way it is. Maybe I'm destined to be alone, to always crave something I can never have. Maybe I'm just a monster like my father, like they all say.

It is because of my father that I am in the position I am today. He created this life for me, and when he fell, there was no way out but for me to take the lead. Having the control is addicting—better than sex, really.

But I'll never forget the girl who tipped the scale in my favor. The girl who shot my father in cold blood and left him bleeding out on the floor of my late mother's bedroom.

She came to uproot our lives. And on the very first day of her stay at our mansion, that is exactly what she did.

Valeria Cipriano.

She is lost to me now. Ran off and disappeared without a trace after her bloody deed. When I find her...I will make her pay for what she did.

Valeria

Four years ago...

"You'll be leaving tomorrow, Valeria. Pack your bags and prepare yourself."

"What?"

"You heard me."

My mouth drops open, but no words come out. I feel my face flush and a knot in my stomach tightens as I gaze at my father incredulously.

"I don't like to repeat myself," he states.

"Well, I don't like being told what to do anymore." My anger surges and with it comes the realization that there is no point in arguing against him.

He laughs. "You're fourteen years old."

"Then why are you giving me away to a man that was once your rival. To Leonardo Argentieri! Why?" I demanded.

"He is no longer my rival. We have made a deal. An impasse if you will...which includes you."

This is something I have feared for so long, yet never expected him to actually follow through on. I want to take a stand and refuse, to tell him that he can't do this to me again, but when I open my mouth nothing but a strangled cry escapes my lips.

My father reclines in his chair. "Whatever happens, the arrangement has been made. You have graduated high school way ahead of your peers, so you will attend university in America until you turn eighteen, and then the Argentieri family will have figured out what use you are to them. From what I understand, they have a son—maybe more than one—so you might not need to marry an old made man after all."

I shake my head. "This is disgusting."

"It ensures your future. Our future." He clasps his hands together. "It ensures...the business. And you are my blood so I expect you to remain loyal when I reach out for your intel."

I finally realize what's in it for him and almost puke.

"You can't do this to me!" I shout.

My father looks at me, his expression unreadable. He calmly responds, "I can, and I am."

I feel my world crumbling around me. I'm going to be leaving my home—again. Father is constantly sending me away. His excuse is that he has no experience raising children, much less a young girl. First, it was boarding school. Now this. The moves are getting old and I can't take it anymore.

Thoughts of fear and uncertainty tumble through my head, and I know I have no choice but to accept my father's wishes, but it doesn't mean I won't try to argue otherwise.

I stare at my father, tears streaming down my face. I can't believe he's doing this to me again. "You sent me away like some kind of property when I was a child, and now you're doing it again? Haven't I suffered enough?" I plead with him, hoping to break through his hardened exterior.

He stretches his arm across the desk, pressing his fingertips into its polished surface. His gaze never falters from mine as he speaks in a measured tone. "You have obligations to fulfill," he said. "A business deal is already in motion with the Argentieri family in New York City, and there's no turning back now. That's all there is to it."

My heart sinks as I realize what this means for me: leaving everything behind and being thrust into an unknown country. But deep down, something stirs within me—a sense of adventure and anticipation for what lies ahead.

"Besides, you'll love New York City since you love to shop so much."

I frown.

My father looks at me with an emotionless face. His eyes, however, tell a different story; he is letting go of me so he can start anew with his new wife and twin boys. My presence has become more of an obligation to him than anything else. To him, I am nothing more than a nuisance.

"Father, please!" I plead with tears streaming down my face.

"The decision is final," he coldly replies.

The guards storm in and grab me by the arms, roughly dragging me towards the door.

"Please listen to me! You can't do this!" I cry out in agony.

"It's time for you to go," Father says, waving his hand dismissively.

As they drag me out of the room, I realize that nothing I say or do will change his mind.

The guards clamp iron hands around my bare arms, their fingertips like hot pokers searing into my skin. They drag me down the hallway, the linoleum tiles cold beneath my feet. The heavy wooden door to my bedroom opens with a hollow thud and I'm pushed inside.

One of the men releases me and hands me a suitcase with a tarnished silver lock. As I survey my room, my eyes fill with tears at all that has been taken away from me.

As the guards shut the door behind them, I realize that I'm being kicked out of my own home—no matter how much I plead or beg for mercy, all hope seems lost.

"Fine," I mumble to myself. "I'll leave this place." And I turn to the door and scream, "Don't expect me to come back when you need me!"

I ran to my dresser, shoveling everything inside—shirts and pants, posters from when I was younger, photographs of my family. My suitcase expanded until it was full, yet none of these things could fill the emptiness in my heart.

Tears stream down my face as the reality of what is happening sets in. I have no one to turn to; my mother died four years ago, and my father remarried. His new wife doesn't care about me, and now even my own father is abandoning me. He didn't even give me a chance to explain myself or prove that I could take care of myself.

I curl up on my bed, clutching my suitcase tightly as I sob into the darkness surrounding me. I feel so helpless, so alone in this moment—there's no point in fighting this. Whether I want it or not, I have to leave behind everything I know and start a new life in New York City with a family I only hear rumors about. I know they are no better than my father—made men who live life on the edge.

My heart heavy with emotions, I slowly stand up from my bed and wipe away the tears staining my cheeks. Taking a deep breath, I determinedly square my shoulders. But deep down, I know that this isn't what I want. I don't want to leave my home, my friends, my life. I don't want to be abandoned by my own father.

I realize that I have no say in the matter. I'm just a pawn in a game that I never asked to play.

Three

Valeria

I awake in the middle of the night, disoriented and confused. I blink my eyes, trying to adjust to the low light of the room. My maid, Rosa, a woman I have known since childhood, is standing next to my bed, a somber expression on her face.

"Miss Valeria," she says softly, her voice heavy with urgency. "You must leave right away. There's a helicopter waiting for you outside."

I try to make sense of what is going on, but my mind is still foggy. "Why? What's happening?" I ask, my heart racing.

"There's no time to explain," she says, taking my arm and helping me out of bed. "You have to come with me now."

I stumble as I try to put on my shoes, my movements clumsy with sleep. She moves quickly, helping me to gather my suitcase.

My stomach churns and twists like a wrung out towel as cold dread washes over me. I try to push it away, but the wretched feeling that something is terribly wrong will not ease.

My father's enraged bellows stand out among them, and I can tell he is already intoxicated. The deep-throated bark of rottweilers near the gates fills my ears and I find myself rooted to the spot, unable to move forward as dread pools in my stomach.

The maid yanks me by the arm, her face a mask of terror, and urges me out the back door in a tumultuous flurry. My feet stumble over each other as we race down the stairs, while the menacing shouting behind us grows in volume with every step. The deafening sound of gunshots reverberates throughout the house, putting a chill down my spine with each terrifying blast. A sense of dread washes over me as I realize that this is no longer an uncommon occurrence in my home. The door slams shut, leaving us barely a breath of a chance to escape. But my heart is pounding with an indomitable will to fight and survive.

I follow her out into the night, the moonlight illuminating our path as we make our way to the awaiting helicopter. We step outside and I see it waiting for me on the pad.

The *thwap-thwap-thwap* of the rotors echo through the trees as the helicopter roars . This isn't one of my father's personal helicopters, sleek and polished to a perfect shine. No, this one is emblazoned with the symbol of our once rival family, the Argentieri's—a grim omen that spells trouble.

Rumor has it that my father owed the Argentieri's a large sum and continually delayed paying them, until they gave him an ultimatum. That's when he agreed to the terms of trading me among other things for his debt. To this day, I don't know what those other things are and I doubt I'll ever know.

The Argentieri emblem glints in the harsh moonlight, taunting me like a dare. Gripping the suitcase with both hands, fear and confusion wash over me as I stare at the Cipriano patch sewn onto it. My stomach churns as I realize what my father has done and why I'm here. Every part of me screams for me to turn back, yet a primal force entices me forward, my destiny inescapable. A chill runs through my veins as I sense impending doom. I clench my eyes tight, feeling helpless against the force that is pushing me closer and closer to the edge. My legs buckle beneath me as desperation and terror wash over me in waves.

Rosa grabs my arm firmly and whispers in my ear, "Valeria, you must go now. This is your only chance to escape." She looks into my eyes with an intensity that tells me that she has been through this before. "Trust me," she continues softly. "Your life depends on it."

I have steeled myself for this moment. I know it is inevitable, so there is no point in fighting any longer. I remain quiet and let her guide me to the waiting helicopter. Step by step, I make my way towards it like a condemned prisoner, feeling as if my feet are encased in blocks of cement that drag behind me with each movement.

As if conjured from the depths of hell, a large, menacing figure appears before us. His thickly tattooed arms reach out in an instant and he grabs me with a vicious grip, squeezing my arm until I whimper in pain. With eyes blazing like fire, he growls at the maid beside me, "Hand her over!"

"What's your problem?" Rosa comes to my defense. "She is *una principessa*. Treat her with respect."

The tattooed guy roars with laughter, mocking and deriding me as if I'm nothing more than a mere peasant compared to his power. The sound of his boisterous guffaw is like thunder clouds rolling over my life, a reminder of the darkness that lurks beneath my status as a mafia princess.

I strain against the tight grasp of the guards, my eyes wide with fear and desperation. Despite my struggles, I'm forced onto the frigid helicopter, leaving the ground far below me.

My body trembles in terror, my heart pounding like a jackhammer inside my chest as I ascend higher and higher into the sky.

My heart is racing faster than my mind can comprehend and I struggle to take a single breath. The guy with the tattered clothes beside me jeers, his face tattooed with a wicked smirk. "Looks like the little princess is having a panic attack, better give her something to calm her down." Fear ripples through me as he leans in closer while taking something from his pocket.

A sharp and merciless prick pierces my skin, driving a need so intense that it feels like needles made of fire are tearing through my flesh. The world starts to spin around me as the poison spreads, searing and burning every nerve in my body until I can feel nothing but agonizing pain. As darkness envelopes me, my mind begins to spiral out of control, consumed by an all-consuming fear of falling from great heights.

I'm left with nothing but the thought that this is the end of everything I've ever known as I plunge into absolute darkness.

Four

Valeria

My head aches from the flight. I have no idea where I am.

I rub my eyes as I sit upright in the king-size bed; a canopy of red and gold fabric hangs from the ceiling above me and waves gently back and forth.

All around the room are beautiful, expensive things that I don't remember seeing before. The room is grand, with a fireplace at one end, softly crackling with a warm, gentle fire. A large bed is positioned near the glass windows directly opposite the fireplace and to my right.

Gold drapery frames each window and gives off a golden glow against the night sky outside. The curtains are drawn shut, obscuring any vision of what lies beyond them.

I slowly take in my surroundings and notice a crest on the bedspread, an 'A' with a crown upon it. It brings me back to reality and I remember what brought me here: the arranged bullshit between me and Leonardo Argentieri, the man my father had sold me to. Fear and distress flood through me, and I'm unable to keep my legs from trembling or stifle the sob that escapes my throat.

No one will come for me. I don't even know if it's because they can't. I had heard the shots before the helicopter took me away and I still have no idea what it all means. If my family is safe. If I'll ever see them again.

I stand up and look around the bedroom. There is a large wardrobe in the corner of the room. It has glass doors, which I slide open to see what it contains. The dark wood gleams on the inside, and several pairs of high heels are arranged at the bottom. A dresser with a large mirror stands beside it. The enormous dresser is covered in small bottles of glittering mosaic glass. The reflections from the light bounce off the colored pieces, like a rainbow at night. Several expensive paintings hang on the walls. I stand before the tall, narrow windows and reach out my hand to test the strength of the iron bars. They are cold to the touch and sink deep into the frames, preventing any chance of escape.

I feel trapped, and I know that there is no escape. I am at the mercy of Leonardo Argentieri, and the thought terrifies me. I have only met the man twice in my life. Once my father invited him to a dinner party my mother hosted in Italy. I was nine. That was when she was alive, of course. If she were still here, she would not agree to this. My father would've listened. The second time I saw him was on a more informal occasion. I was eleven—had just been sent off to the boarding school. Leonardo visited the boarding school. A young boy was with him—maybe his son. But the boy, with dark hair and brooding eyes, stood about two heads taller than Leonardo. I would later learn that Leonardo had attempted to enroll a son who wasn't accepted. I guess money couldn't buy all things after all.

Money certainly will not buy my freedom right now. Even if I had access to my trust fund, which I didn't because I wasn't eighteen years old yet, I wouldn't know where to begin. I'm just a fourteen year old stupid girl with no one. I lie back down on the bed, tears streaming down my face, wondering how I am going to survive this nightmare.

As I lie there, I hear footsteps coming down the hallway, and my heart starts racing. I know that whoever is coming is not friendly—none of the Argentieris are apparently—and I need to find a way out. I jump out of bed and race to the door, but it is still locked. I hear the footsteps getting closer, but then they move pass. I release my breath.

I look around the room for anything I can use to escape, but everything is too heavy or too fragile. I know that I have to take my chances and try to run. I decide to climb out of the window, but when I try to open the only one with no bars, it won't budge.

I frantically rifle through the nightstand and grab a pen. I attempt to insert it into the keyhole of the door. After a few failed attempts, I hear a faint click as the lock releases. Slowly, I push open the door and peek out into the hallway; thankfully, it is deserted.

I tiptoe down two flights of stairs, the echo of each footstep ringing in my ears. When I reach the bottom, I spot a pair of double doors at the far end of the hall. I make a break for it and fling them open, only to be met by complete silence and an array of cold stares. At the head of the table sits Leonardo Argentieri, his lips pressed into a thin line.

My heart skips a beat when I step into the room and my gaze comes to rest on the four men seated there. A younger version of Leonardo sits to his left. His hair is a shade or two darker than Leonardo and he has the same brooding eyes as the boy I saw with Leonardo at the boarding school all those years ago. It's his son. I know his name now—Dante. He was slumping over when I barged in but now his back is straight and his gaze focuses on me. The other three men have their eyes fixed on me too, one sporting a thick gray mustache and two more in black suits. I feel like my feet are glued to the floor, like if I move I'll set off an unseen alarm. Not a sound can be heard as we stare at each other in complete silence.

"Fucking stupid bitch!" Leonardo stands up. "What are you doing in here?"

"You disrespectful asshole! How dare you keep me locked away in a fucking room?" I can feel the rage bubbling up inside me, my voice echoing around the walls. Every muscle in my body vibrates with fury at Leonardo's control, and I know that only he holds the power here.

"Take this bitch back to her room right now!" Leonardo demands. "I'm in a business meeting."

More guards than seems possible appears out of the shadows, and one of them clamps a vice-like grip onto my arm so tight that I swear I can hear bones creaking. The guard marches me back upstairs as I scream with all my might, my voice reverberating louder than thunder through the air and echoing off the walls like a banshee's wail.

If they want me here against my will, I will show them what they have gotten themselves into. Maybe then Leonardo will send me back to Italy.

I don't belong here. I'm not meant for this family. I'm a Cipriano princess, not an Argentieri bastard.

Five

Valeria

The two men, both much larger than me, had firm grips on my arms as I scream and curse. My pleas for freedom are ignored, and I feel a wave of hopelessness wash over me as they shut the door. I slump to the ground, surrounded by four walls that now feels like a prison. I am left alone in the room, feeling hopeless and trapped.

The door creaks open and a petite maid scurries in, her arms laden with a tray of bright colored sliced fruit, cold cuts, pasta, and the smell of freshly baked pastries. There's a guard waiting outside the door. I can see him peering in, probably to make sure I don't cause another scene.

"Please," I beg. "I need a phone."

The maid shakes her head. "I can't help you with that, but I can prepare any dish you want."

"I don't even know how long I've been here. I need to get in touch with my family," I plead.

"He will be angry," she warns. "If you start trouble, it will only come back to bite you in the end," she cautions, as she pours a glass of juice and sets it on a small table in front of the bed.

Fury surges through me at the thought of being stuck here at the mercy of Leonardo. If I want a chance of going home, I have to take a risk and anger him. I have already made up my mind about it; I am desperate to get out of there and willing to take the risk if it means finding a way back home.

The maid, ignoring my tears and protests, firmly leaves the room and I am so hungry I start eating the food. Everything is good, but that isn't the point. I don't want to be here.

Just as I am finishing up the soup and staring down at the remaining rolls of salami on the plate, Leonardo barges into the room. He looks angrier than ever before, and I know that I am in trouble.

He is a huge old man, bigger than my father. His domineering nature strikes fear in me as it would any teenage girl faced with this situation.

"You'll pay for making me look like a fool in front of all those bosses," he snarls, his eyes burn right through me.

I feel a chill down my spine. There is no mistaking the menacing tone of his voice. I sense this is going to get ugly and I have to find a way out. Fast.

"I'm sorry," I say, getting up from the table and backing a few feet away. "I didn't mean to embarrass you."

He glares at me through narrowed eyes and crosses his arms, his rage all too apparent. "You don't get it," he spits. "I don't care what your intentions were. You should have known better! You're a mafia princess, are you not?"

I sigh and nod, knowing there's no reasoning with him now. I have angered him. Whenever I angered my father, he would always just send me away as punishment, but this man wasn't my father and it doesn't look like he's going to just send me off.

"If you think you're going to come to America from Italy and act like an insipid little bitch, you've got another thing coming," he shouts.

Leonardo's voice grows ever louder as he criticizes me, and I can feel the weight of his words bearing down on my body. I clench my teeth together and curl my hands into tight fists as he incessantly continues to reprimand me. Until at last, a strange force compels me to stand up for myself. If I set the precedent now, maybe, just maybe these Argentieris will respect me.

"That's enough", I insist, lifting my chin and challenging his seething eyes. "I'm tired of taking orders from old men like you." My voice trembles with rage. "I want to be free. Not here. Not treated like a prisoner in a cage."

His cruel laughter rings in my ears like a malignant bell and then he grabs my arms and jerks me up against him. "You don't understand, do you? You belong to me now to do as I see fit. That means if I want you in a cage you will be in a cage. You have no power over your own fate because your daddy signed that away to me. You will obey without question!" His words hit me like a sharp blow and the fear in my heart grows ever stronger.

I have to find a way out, no matter what it takes. I know that I have to be strong, and that I have to keep fighting until I find a way to escape this nightmare.

So, I continue to scream and curse at him, hoping that someone will hear me and come to my rescue. I know that I have to keep fighting, no matter what the consequences. And with that thought in mind, I brace myself for whatever is to come.

Suddenly, Leonardo looks down at my cleavage and begins to touch me inappropriately. I know this is wrong. Father said that things wouldn't go this way until I was eighteen.

He wouldn't have lied about that, and if father knew what Leonardo was about to do to me...

I felt a wave of panic come over me as his hands started exploring my body with no regard for my feelings or comfort.

"Stop," I mutter.

"I will ruin you just like your father ruined my business deal for me. This is the price he must pay for it," he grunts.

I shudder in revulsion as he starts making lewd comments and continues to grope me despite all my struggles. Tears fill up my eyes but there's nobody around who could help me escape the horror unfolding before me.

"Do as I command or I will go down to Italy and blow the brains out of everyone you love," he hissed. "I might not be able to turn you into a housewife, but I can turn you into a *whore.*"

Leonardo notices the fear in my eyes, and it only fuels him further. He pulls me closer in an effort to take control and I can feel his breath on my face—hot, angry breaths that reek of alcohol and cigarettes. His fingers start tugging at the neckline of my dress, as if he can't wait any longer for what he thinks is rightfully his—access to a young woman's body without permission or consequence.

I inhale slowly, each breath attempting to calm a different limb of my jittering body. Leonardo wraps his fingers around my neck and squeezes hard.

"Please stop!" I scream. They are loud enough for others to hear on any level, but I doubt anyone will come help me now.

As I try to formulate an escape plan, the door slams open with the force of a lightning bolt, lodging it against the wall. In thundering footsteps, Leonardo's son, Dante charges inside. "Father!" The shockwave of sound reverberates off every surface and pierces my eardrums like hot needles.

My heart cannonballs into my throat as adrenaline floods my veins. My gaze lock onto Dante, and I take in the sight of him, the dark-haired Adonis with the brooding eyes. His powerful frame is draped in a fine suit, chiseled jawline and piercing eyes making his presence known.

"What are you doing, Father?" Dante repeats.

Leonardo instantly loosens his grip on me, turns around, and his eyes shoot to his son.

"What the fuck do you want, son?" Leonardo asks, his voice seething with anger.

Dante seems to be unaffected by his father's aggression as he stands his grounds. "The others are waiting, father."

"For what?" Leonardo closes the distance between himself and Dante.

Dante looks down at the ground. "Your decision."

Leonardo explodes with rage, and slaps his son across the face. Dante doesn't budge, whimper, or cry out. He barely moves a muscle.

Leonardo roars with anger, "Have you no spine, boy! I taught you to take the lead, and yet here you stand with nothing but insolence in your veins. Make a decision that will make me proud!"

"Yes, Father." Dante whips out a handkerchief and holds it over his bleeding nose before turning away and disappearing as fast as he appeared.

I am horrified by the violence and brutality of it all. I am still shivering in the corner, still stiff from the previous altercation. I can see the resemblance between the two, and I can't help but think they're all violent monsters.

Leonardo approaches me, and I try to push him away, but he grabs me by the arms and pins me against the wall. I struggle to break free, but his grip is too strong. I know he's going to take his anger out on me now.

My mind races with thoughts of escape, but I can't seem to find a way out. My heart sinks as I realize that I am trapped once again.

He yanks on my dress and rips it in half and then throws me on the bed. "Women are more obedient when they've been broken," he grunts.

He stands over me and then he's on the bed.

There's a scuffle between us and his handgun drops from his belt. I grab it as he's driving a hard knee between my legs, trying to get me to open wide.

In the heat of the moment, I try to kick his balls, hoping to get him off me but the gun is in my hand and my finger engages the trigger. I hear a loud *pfft*—a gunshot muffled by a silencer. *Oh God.*

Leonardo stands up grabbing his torso with a stoic expression on his face and his mouth gaps open. Blood begins to stain through his white dress shirt. He slumps to the floor on his knees like someone succumbing to his master, bleeding profusely, and then keels over.

My hands are shaking as I realize what I've done. I let go of the hard object in my hand. It's the gun. It falls to the floor.

I've shot a man.

Adrenaline surges through my veins as everything after that becomes a blur. I burst out of the house, past the guards and maids screaming in pursuit. My feet pound on the ground as I frantically seek to put more distance between me and the chaos left behind. Despite my haste, confusion clouds my mind, leaving me completely disoriented; every thought ravaged by recent events, unable to think clearly despite my desperate need for a plan.

I've been running so much suddenly I see homeless people on the side of the street begging for money. I didn't realize it before, but I'm half naked—down to my underwear. At least I'm alive, but my heart sinks as I realize just how lost and alone I am now. I stumble into some kind of building—almost like a soup kitchen where people were lined up wearing large shoulder bags and rolling around shopping carts filled with trash, plastic bottles, and bent hubcaps. I stumble up to the door exhausted...and then it's light out for me.

Six

Dante

Present Day...

The polished metal and mirrored walls of the elevator seem to close in on me as I step inside, my two bodyguards forming a tight triangle around me. Vito, my underboss, stands in front with his hands clasped behind his back, staring into the empty space ahead. Vito pressed the button for the twentieth floor and the car slowly lurches upwards.

We're on our way to visit one of my clients, a man who owned a trucking company among other businesses and owes me an assload of money. He had been dodging my calls for weeks. But two things I know he can't dodge for long—me or bullets.

The elevator dings and the doors open, revealing a luxurious hallway lined with expensive artwork and designer furniture. We make our way to the door of my client's suite and Vito knocks firmly.

After a moment, the door opens and Nigel stands before us, looking anxious. I can tell he knows why we're here. There's a white powdery substance all over his nose and mustache and he looks high as a kite.

"Mr. Argentieri, I wasn't expecting you this evening. But, please come in," he says, stepping aside to let us in.

We enter the spacious living room and take seats on the leather couches. Nigel makes no attempts to hide the drug paraphernalia on his glass coffee table and sits across from us, fidgeting nervously.

"I've been meaning to call you, Mr. Argentieri. I just needed a little more time to come up with the money," he says, his voice shaking.

"How much more time?" I ask, my tone calm but firm.

"Another week, maybe two," he says, avoiding eye contact.

"Time ran out two weeks ago. Money is due now," I say.

"I understand, but I'm doing everything I can," he says, desperation creeping into his voice. "I...I've got some guys on it."

I lean forward in my seat and Nigel shrank back.

"Nigel, I needed you to understand something and needed you to understand it the moment you borrowed from me. Your cash was due net 30 days and you're already in arrears with interest. You don't have my product. You don't have my cash. And—" I state.

"—wait! I-I have it. I have some of it." Nigel jumps up and goes over to his desk where he pulls out a key, which I suspect opens his safe.

I exchange a glance with Vito, and he nods. Vito and the others get up and drag Nigel all the way over to the safe. When it's opened all I see are bags of cocaine and one stack of bills. I'm not amused at all.

I watch as my client's face turns pale. "It was here. It was just here. Someone must have stolen from me," Nigel stammers as Vito grips him by the collar.

"Cut the crap," I say, my voice rising.

Vito slams Nigel's head against the safe, causing him to yelp in pain.

"I want my fucking money, Nigel," I say, no longer masking my anger.

Nigel whimpers and looks up at me with pleading eyes. "Please, Mr. Argentieri, I'll get it to you. I swear. Just give me a little more time."

I stand up and walk over to Nigel, towering over him. "You've had enough time. You had your chance to make things right, and now you've only made things worse for yourself by sitting around snitching and sniffing."

"I don't know what you mean," Nigel exclaims.

"You've been snitching to the cops. You know what happens to snitches, and I can't have someone like that owing me money," I say, my voice rising.

"I swear I haven't said anything," he says, his voice shaking.

I stand up, my fists clenched. "I don't believe you," I say, grabbing him by the collar of his shirt.

He tries to pull away, but my bodyguards hold him in place. I can see the fear in his eyes.

"I'll do anything, please don't hurt me," he begs.

"You're going to tell me everything you know," I say, my voice cold. "Why you fucking snitched to the cops and who put that hit out on me last month."

My piercing stare bore into Nigel, demanding the truth.

"W-what hit?" Nigel's voice trembles as he nervously replies.

"Enough with the games, Nigel," I growl, my voice icy. "Give me names. Details."

Nigel's eyes dart around the room, seeking solace in the shadows. Finally, he exhales sharply, his voice shaky as he reveals the hidden truth.

"Vincent Moretti. He's the one who ordered the hit on you," Nigel confesses, his words barely above a whisper. "He operates from an old warehouse near the riverfront."

My eyes narrow, my fists clench with fury. Moretti is an old associate of mine. We fell out when I wouldn't let him into my circle and then he came crying to me like a pussy about it. It was just like him to send someone after and not come himself.

"Vincent Moretti," I repeat, my voice dripping with menace. "He will soon regret crossing my path again. Tell me everything, Nigel."

Nigel takes a cautious step backward, his fear palpable. "He's at a warehouse. Where I store my trucks. T-the w-warehouse is heavily guarded. He's got the Stoner gang guarding him."

A predatory smile plays on my lips as my resolve grows stronger. "You mean the gang that supplies your coke."

Nigel's eyes grow wide. He doesn't know that I know that he's been double crossing everyone. Switching sides just to stay alive and causing more problems than what it's worth.

Nigel trembles visibly, morbid etching his face. "Please..." he begs.

I shake my head, sighing heavily. "Pussies I can deal with, Nigel. But snitches...I can't have that."

"H-how did you know?" he croaks out.

I slip a tape recorder out of my inside pocket and hit the play button. "This you?"

Nigel's voice was loud and clear as he tattled to the police about any valuables that I might have been keeping hidden in a foreign country offshore.

Nigel curses under his breath. He knows he's doomed. Snitching on a man he owes money to to save his own ass. Of course he is.

I signal to Vito, who pulls out a gun and points it at Nigel's head. Nigel's eyes widen as he realizes what's about to happen.

"Wait, please!" Nigel pleads, but Vito pulls the trigger. The sound of the gunshot echoes through the room, followed by the sickening thud of Nigel's body hitting the ground.

I turn to my remaining bodyguards. "Clean this up. We're done here."

"And about Moretti?" Vito says.

"He'll be dead by tomorrow," I reply, stepping over the lifeless body of Nigel.

As I make my way back to the elevator, I can't help but wonder how many more times I'll have to do this to double-crossing bastards. But in this business, these are the things I do to survive this ruthless business. If not anything else, my father taught me this. In fact, he once told me that I'd thank him for all the times he broke me down just so I could get back up and become stronger.

Too bad he can't see me now because I am a different man because of him.

Seven

Valeria

I stare blankly at the computer screen, trying to focus on the task at hand. The text blurs and I rub my eyes with weariness. Four years had passed since I escaped Leonardo's grasp, but the memories still haunted me.

The new listing for the Italian-style mansion triggered a vivid memory of the night I fought for my freedom. Sharp images of crouching in the corner as an old man stared down at me, hearing screams, breaking glass, and gunshots, and the taste of metal on my tongue as I bit down to keep from crying out flooded my senses. Even years later, I can still feel the anguish radiating through my body.

I inhale, feeling my chest swell and the air filling my lungs. I've found techniques to deal with my anxiety. But it never manages to push away the memories.

I spent months in a homeless shelter, living off scraps and scheduled meals. Thank God I am a woman because the shelter manager would always make sure I had a place to lay my head each night. I can still feel the chill of terror freezing my veins when I heard whispers of the Argentieri family looking for me. They had hired hitmen to track me down, so I was constantly on the move, seeking new hideouts.

The streets weren't easy, but I had hid for months with no source of income until a kind woman hired me in one of her clothing boutiques. I worked there for three years until the owner finally retired and moved to south France. I found my way to real estate school and now I am working at a job that I don't hate so much. It is kind of easy convincing people that they should buy nice big pretty houses.

Every night, sleep evaded me as I stayed awake, pacing back and forth, wondering if there would ever come a time when I could truly rest. And then there was the guilt. The guilt of shooting Leonardo in self-defense. I heard that he had passed away at the hospital; it was all on the news, but back then I couldn't bring myself to turn myself in, knowing that I would face the wrath of a mob of merciless mafia families for killing their *Capo di Tutti Capi*. I can't even bring myself to do it now.

But the worst news was yet to come after that. The day I found out that my entire family had been murdered back in Italy the same night the helicopter took me away, I had thought my life was over too. The thought of them being wiped out, just like that, still brings tears to my eyes.

I couldn't even get revenge for their deaths because I was in hiding myself. The thought of my family's murderers walking free, unpunished, fills me with anger and frustration. There are no whispers in America about who killed my father, Marco Cipriano. The crime had been committed in Italy and his death likely only affected the mob families there. People like the Argentieris would've gained nothing from my father's death—or at least that's what I thought and what I still think. Either way, I still crave the truth...even if it will put me in harm's way.

Amanda, the receptionist's voice jolts me back to reality. I look up from the glossy brochures that are strewn across the desk.

"Can you do a showing in an hour for this big buyer who is ready to pay cash?" she asks, her eyebrows raised and her voice eager.

"I think so," I mumble, looking at my calander.

Before I can confirm, Amanda says, "Good. I'll tell Mr. Jones you'll be there."

"Wait..." My heart sinks as I remember my appointment at the post office—I've finally saved enough money to take that trip out of the country and now it seems like this sale will get in the way.

"So much for my trip," I groan. "There's always tomorrow." My mind is already set on going to Italy. I need to find out who killed my family and why. I need answers, closure. Even if those answers get me killed.

My fingers flew over my laptop as I rebooked my flight. As I head out the door, I can feel the weight of the memories and the uncertainty of what lies ahead weighing heavily on my shoulders.

As I drive to the property, the only sound I hear is the low rumble of my engine and my own heart beating in my chest. The weight of my decision presses down on me like a boulder, threatening to crush me at any moment. Going back to Italy could put me in danger, but I can't let the fear control me anymore. My eyes flicker up to the rearview mirror every few seconds as if I'm being followed. The road stretches ahead of me like an endless ribbon, twisting and turning through the mountains until finally, I see it—my destination. It's a old villa nestled among rolling hills.

I park my car, switch from my flats to stilettos, and step out into the crisp air. I can't shake off this feeling that something terrible is about to happen, especially if I take that flight to Italy. But despite all of this, I know what I have to do: face my demons head-on.

Eight

Dante

I sit in my car, watching Valeria Cipriano from across the street. It's been months since I discovered where she works and lives. I have been watching her. Every time I see her, the anguish I feel is almost unbearable. Valeria is the one who got away and she almost destroyed everything. She's the reason my father is gone, the reason I was thrust into this life of power and responsibility.

At twenty, I was dubbed the new mafia king. At twenty-one, I already had more assets to my name than most men twice my age. And now, four years later, I still feel unfulfilled and encumbered by everything hanging over my head—all because of her.

I didn't plan this. My father was supposed to remain capo di tutti i capi for the duration of his life. I had my own business ventures carved out. I had never ruled out affiliation with the mob but I always wanted something for myself—something I, and only I, create.

Valeria Cipriano. The name alone is enough to make my blood boil. The image of her sweet smile and seductive eyes still haunts me to this day. Most nights, her bedroom gaze and soft brown hair with glimmering streaks of gold take over my dreams.

She's beautiful, I'll give her that. And I imagine she probably sweet-talked her way into my father's bedroom like all the other women in his life—including my mother. But unlike them, she got away. She got away with it all.

My anger towards her is not just because of what she did to my father, but because of what she represents. She's a reminder of my weaknesses, my failures. I should have been able to prevent what happened to my father, but I was too naive, too trusting. And now I'm left with this burden, this weight on my shoulders that I can never shake off.

But there's something else that's been gnawing at me, something that's been impeding my ability to exact revenge on her. It's a feeling that I'm not used to, a feeling that I can't quite put my finger on. But I can't afford to let that feeling cloud my judgment, not when there's so much at stake.

Anyway, I imagine seeing her beg for her life at my feet. I imagine sliding all nine inches of my dick down her throat and watching her swallow my load. I want to ruin her—the Cipriano princessa—for all other men.

I take a deep breath and try to push those thoughts aside. Valeria Cipriano is my enemy, and I will stop at nothing to make her pay for what she's done.

I watch as she slips into a little red BMW and drives off, her wavy long hair catching the light of the setting sun. My black heart twists as I see her go. How dare she live a life of normalcy, of freedom, while I'm trapped in this gilded cage of my own making.

"Boss, she's on the move. Follow her?" the driver, Nolen, asks from the front seat.

"No, head to the property," I say, my voice cold and detached.

Valeria Cipriano never paid her debt, neither before or after she shot my father. Argentieri men always collect what they're owed.

Nine

Valeria

I nervously tap my foot as I glance at the time on my wristwatch. After thirty minutes, not a single person has shown up yet. A growing feeling of dread overcomes me; I should've known better than to agree to this meeting. I let out an exasperated sigh as I grab my phone and dial the listing office.

Amanda answers.

"Hi Amanda, this is Valeria speaking," I said. "The prospective buyer hasn't arrived yet. Can you please page Mr. Jones for me?"

"Sure."

I wait through hold music for about three minutes and then Mr. Jones picks up the phone. "Hey Valeria, what's going on?"

"Who's the client? They're not here yet and it's been thirty minutes," I say, shifting from foot to foot. I'm thinking about saying to hell with it and kicking off these stilettos. People should at least have the decency to respect others' time.

"Give him fifteen more minutes, Val. This is a very important client," Mr. Jones says.

I sigh in frustration and hang up the phone. Fifteen more minutes and then I'm out of here.

A car pulls up in the driveway, and I get a bad feeling in the pit of my stomach. I grab my black tote bag, making sure my mace and my weapon are within easy reach. I'm not taking any chances.

I peak out through the blinds. The car windows are all tinted, so I can't see who's inside. Two men in black suits get out of the car. One opens the back passenger side door. My hand grips the edge of the window sill as memories flood back—memories that I've tried my hardest to forget. I consider running out the backdoor and disappearing forever, but something inside me tells me to stay put. The air thickens with anticipation as a familiar figure steps out of the car.

As the black sedan door creaks open, my heart pounds like a timpani drum. A giant of a man steps out, hulking and ominous even from this distance. Without thinking, my fingers clench around the strap of my purse until they feel like they might snap. It's him—Dante Argentieri, son of the infamous Leornardo Argentieri. Known for his mercilessness and towering stature, he is a force to be reckoned with.

Oh fuck. He knows...

He's found me.

Maybe not. Maybe it's just a coincidence.

Maybe he won't recognize me—my hair has changed a lot in the last few years. I chopped it into a pixie cut four years ago, and dyed it a golden blonde color. After that it had grown out just past my shoulders. All traces of the blonde has since faded away, and now my natural hair color is back.

I'm not a girl anymore; I'm a woman. Even though I've only seen photos or heard rumors about Dante over the years, he still seems to exude the same malicious vibes. It's like he's stayed exactly the same as his younger self except for growing into a full grown man. He is truly the devil in disguise.

He slowly approaches the entranceway, and I involuntarily back away, feeling like a caged animal. I was uncertain of who he was or why he had come. There was no way to know if this was whom I was supposed to be meeting today. All I could be sure of is that I needed to remain vigilant and on guard. He wouldn't exact revenge here, would he? I could try and disguise my accent, but I'm not very good at it. As my anxiety increases, I force myself to take a deep breath in order to steady my nerves and think logically. Running out the back door seems like the better idea.

Someone knocks on the door frame and my heart just about jumps out of my chest. The doorbell works, but one of his bodyguards choose to bang the knocker like an idiot.

My breathing becomes labored and I bump up against the rigid marble table in the entryway.

I can't do this. I just can't.

Too late.

The door swings open as if on it's own accord, but I know that can't be true because the door is armed with a code. I'm not sure if it was rigged or if I neglected to lock it properly.

Dante strides across the threshold, and I feel like I'm about to die—my heart stops, my breath catches in my throat. He's here and nothing else matters. His stone-cold expression reveals his intention, and I'm sure that this is the end for me. His eyes are dark and cold, and there's a dangerous aura around him. I know I'm in trouble.

"Ms. Cipriano," he says, his voice low and menacing. "It's time for us to have a little chat."

I swallow hard, my mouth dry. This isn't good. I know I should have listened to my gut. I might have been down the street by now. In my car. Getting the hell out of dodge. But now, it's too late. I'm face to face with the one man I never wanted to see again.

Ten

Valeria

I'm rooted to the spot as Dante strides through the doorway, his frame so massive it blots out the light from outside. I grip my bag with shaking fingers, feeling my heart stutter in my chest. My tongue is glued to the roof of my mouth and no matter how hard I try, the words stuck in my throat refuse to come out. Terror claws at me, threatening to drag me further into the abyss.

"What do you want?" I manage to choke out.

"I'm here to view the home," he replies, his voice smooth and calm. "But I thought you already knew that."

My heart races as I realize he can't be telling the truth. Every fiber of my being screams at me in warning, realizing that this was no coincidence. His presence here confirms his sinister intentions—he has been tracking my every move. Adrenaline floods my veins and a paralyzing fear takes hold as panic rises within me.

"You've been following me," I hiss, my heart pounding in my chest.

"I don't deny it." He meets my gaze.

He keeps coming closer and closer until his bodyguards flank him on either side.

"Why are you even here?" I demand, digging my hand through my purse. I pull out my weapon. "Stay back. All of you."

"What are you going to do?" Dante's mouth twitched in an ironic smirk as he chuckles. "Take us out one by one?"

My finger slides dangerously close to the hammer as I use my free hand to pull out my cell phone.

Dante doesn't even flinch. He asks, "You're not going to call the police on me now, are you?"

I can barely speak. "I...I want you to leave. I'll do what I have to."

"It would be a shame and a travesty if you were to end up in an orange jumpsuit," he says, his eyes fixed on me.

I feel a chill run down my spine and, without thinking, I lift the gun higher to aim for his head. Two hulking bodyguards with hands on their holsters step in front of him, ready to intervene.

Dante holds up a hand to stop them. "Stand down," he says softly, but firmly. "Leave us."

The guard hesitates before reluctantly taking a few steps back, but he keeps his gaze trained on me. With an unyielding look, Dante repeats himself more forcefully: "Leave. Us."

They leave.

My heart races as I watch Dante slowly make his way around the room, seemingly unbothered by the gun I had trained on him. He seems so calm and fearless in the face of death, yet I couldn't help feeling an odd sense of familiarity that makes me hesitant to pull the trigger.

The phone's shrill ring echoes through the empty space. My grip relaxes on the gun as I ponder whether to answer. It's likely someone who can help me or alert the cops that I've been stalked and cornered by a mob boss.

"Well answer it," he says as he glances up at me with a sly smirk. "It should be Mr. Jones."

My mouth opens in shock. How did he know my boss's name?

I fish the phone back out of my purse and I'm in surprise to find that it is Mr. Jones.

"Hello?" I said, my voice quivering.

"Good news," my boss bellows on the other end. "The purchase is complete and Dante will be taking the keys from you."

I had to take a moment to process it.

"You made a quick and easy sale," he continues. "The bonus will be quite nice. Congratulations."

Before I can even respond, he had already hung up the phone.

I turn to Dante, confused and scared. "What have you done?" I ask.

Dante grins slowly. "I've just become the proud owner of this fine mansion...and...well...everything in it, including *you.*"

Before I can react, there's a blur of motion and someone bumps into me from behind. I spin around before I can think. A large hand clamps my shoulder to the wall, then wraps around my neck. Three men crowd in close, each with a gun in his hand. My heart pounds against my chest and the adrenaline kicks in, turning my mind to mush.

Hands smother my mouth and eyes while I'm lifted up into the air. My feet leave the ground and I struggle against the tight grip until my body slams onto hard leather seats. A sudden realization of my captivity settles on me like a heavy rock in the pit of my stomach.

I'm at Dante's mercy now, and I have no idea what he has planned for me.

Eleven

Valeria

My heart is pounding in my chest as I scream and struggle against the restraints that bind my hands behind my back. I try to kick the car door open, but they won't budge. The soundproof barrier muffles my screams, but I know Dante can hear them. He sits right because me. He ignores me as he argues with someone about a diamond drop.

I'm blindfolded, and I have no idea where we're going. The car jolts and swerves, and all I see through the fabric covering my eyes are flashes of lights and shadows. I'm terrified. I don't know what Dante is planning to do with me, but I fear the worst. Men like him fuck with his victims before they're executed.

What the heck did he want from me besides revenge for his father? He could've had that a long time ago. All he had to do was pull the trigger from afar and I would never know what hit me.

But no, he had to make it personal. He had to drag me into this dark abyss and subject me to a fate worse than death. I want to scream at him, but I know it won't do any good. His cold-heartedness and thirst for revenge don't have any room for mercy or sympathy.

Dante leans over and whispers, "You should know by now that your actions won't earn you any brownie points with me."

"Fuck you!" I exclaim.

"Fine," is his only reply.

Finally, the car comes to a halt, and I hear the driver step out and open the door. I scramble outside, yanking against Dante's grip on my arm. The blindfold is removed, and I blink in the bright moonlight, taking in the sight of a glorious four-story mansion in front of me. It's easily the most beautiful and expensive building I've ever seen. But I don't care about the view. I care about my freedom.

"You fucking scumbags, let me go," I scream out into the night. My voice echoes and a pack of dogs bark in the distance.

The pavements outside are lined with an array of luxurious cars. Each vehicle gleams under the sun, their glossy shells reflecting the light like mirrors. Every car is an opulent masterpiece, proudly displaying golden trimmings and flashy chrome accents. The Argentieri family probably had so much money they didn't know what to do with it. My father always told me they came from old money. Very old money. If they exit the mob business tomorrow, they'd still have enough in investments to live off for generations.

Three heavily tattooed men are waiting for us outside in the courtyard. Two of them are wearing black suits, and the third, a guy in a Hawaiian-themed shirt, walks up and spits on the pavement in front of my bare feet. I'm not wearing heels anymore; they must have gotten lost somewhere in the struggle. My instinct was to cease my screams and outbursts, as I knew the situation was about to become dire.

The one in the Hawaiian shirt speaks up. "Is this the one that killed your father, Dante? The Cipriano bitch, yes?"

His words feel like shards of glass, slicing me deep when he speaks to me in a condescending manner and uses belittling terms.

Without a word, the man in the Hawaiian shirt lashes out at me with searing speed. His hand connects with my face with a resounding crack, sending an uncontrollable wave of agony through my skull. The pain intensifies as I feel warmth flooding from my nose and around my mouth. I'm sure I'll have a monstrous bruise on my face in no time, but that's not the worst of it—I can taste the metallic tang of blood in my mouth.

It's obvious he is mad at me for killing Dante's father, his boss. Was this my fate? Were they going to take turns beating me for what I had done?

Dante whips out his gun from his jacket with a sinister, metallic snick of the silencer. He presses the cold barrel to the dude's forehead and pulls the trigger without hesitation. The gunshot echoes like thunder in my ears as the man in the Hawaiian shirt crumples lifelessly to the ground, his head ruptured by the force of the bullet. Blood had splattered like rain on my white shirt and blazer, some even reaching my face and coating it in a bloody mask.

I exhale a ragged breath, doubling over in anguish.

"I will not tolerate anyone laying a single finger on her. Her fate is mine and mine alone to decide. Do you hear me?!" Dante roared, his voice reverberating off the walls of the alleyway.

His men were aghast, their gazes switching between the dead man at their feet and Dante.

"Understand?" Dante's breath rattles as he roars. "Touch her and you're dead."

They all nod vigorously, and some scatter from the area. A couple stay behind to drag off the body.

I press my palm to my face, trying in vain to mop away the tears streaming down my cheeks. Dante's gaze shifted to me, and in that split second I see something flicker in his face—guilt mixed with a hint of empathy. His eyes harden as the look vanished, leaving behind a stoic mask. His expression shifts yet again, and he turns and motions with two fingers for me to follow him.

Taking a deep breath, I step into the shadow of the towering three-story mansion and fall in line behind him in silence. I am at Dante's mercy.

I will live another day, but tomorrow, who knows...

Twelve

Dante

As I lead Valeria into the grand entrance of the mansion, my thoughts race, conflicting emotions swirling within me like a tempest. She looks so innocent, so pure, and I can't help but wonder if I'm doing anything right by bringing her back into this dangerous world. Is it fair to involve her in my dark affairs? I know the answer, but it doesn't ease the turmoil in my heart. The pain she caused.

After all, my father signed that contract in blood—the one that said she is to be a servant to the Argentieri family for the rest of her natural life. The specifics were not made known to me at the time. I was young then and kept out of that side of my father's dealings—the side which dealt with some nefarious and strange customs thought up by old-time mobsters. But in my four years of taking over for my father, I can understand how a man could make such contracts.

This business is all about sacrifice. Nothing is free. Everyone pays for everything whether it be with money, exchange of power, or through sacrifice. I learned this the hard way and I'm still learning it to this day.

The weight of responsibility settles heavily upon my shoulders. I can't deny the attraction I feel for her which is ten times greater than the hate I feel, the way she lights up the room with her presence even when she's down. But beneath the surface, there's a deeper conflict. Is she just a pawn in my game? A means to an end like all the rest of them? I feel some sort of pride for finally getting her back to where she truly belongs.

Before all of this, before that contract my father made to obtain her, I had seen her only once before. She was in the registration office at some bullshit school in Italy asking about mail from her father. Even then she was a beautiful girl. She probably doesn't even remember it or how she looked at me with so much sadness. It was when my father took me there, trying to buy me a place there because the families were engaged in a bloody war with several cartel street gangs. My uncle had already been killed and he'd lost two lieutenants and his underboss. Word on the street was that I was next on the hit list. I didn't get accepted to the school. I might have known her if I did. My father dragged me all the way back to the States where he sent me to live with my mother's people. I told him I never wanted to go; I would rather die fighting than run off to some land of cattle shit out in the middle of nowhere, but I lost that argument. It took my father a year to settle the score; to run the cartel gangs out of his territory. It took me a year to get back to New York City.

I watch her as she looks around my mansion, taking in the opulence and grandeur of the interior. She's not completely out of her element; she knows this life. She comes from money. I know my family has upended her life, thrusting her into a world on the other side of the Atlantic she never asked for. I heard her people were dead, but why had she not gone back to Italy already? Why did she choose to hide in plain sight?

As we reach a momentary pause by the staircase, our eyes meet. I see confusion mingled with a flicker of defiance in her gaze. She is no ordinary woman. I see a fight in her, and my father wanted her for something, but what?

I point up the stairs, directing her to continue. "Ascend."

"Please," she whispered. "Don't make me go back up there."

She thinks I'm sending her to the same room she shot my father in. My mother's room.

I looked away from her and pointed. "Go. Or you will be carried."

She takes a step up and ascends the spiral staircase. Her hips sashay with each step and I bite my tongue as my dick stirs to life.

The weight of my choices bears down on me as I know I'll need to decide what to do with her. In the moments after my father was shot, his lieutenants were out for blood. Had she been found by them, she would've been dead by a lieutenant's hand a long time ago.

In this mansion of secrets, where power and danger intertwine, I can't help but wonder if Valeria is the key to salvation or the catalyst for my downfall. The conflicting forces within me wage an internal war.

I veer off to the left and open a door to the biggest guest suite. It's not my mother's room where she shot my father. I'd never allow anyone to sleep there. It's off limits.

I grasp the large brass door handle, push it open, and step aside to let her in. She stands on the threshold, her eyes wide as they take in the room. She steps forward tentatively, her head swiveling as she takes in every detail.

"Your clothes..." I point, gesturing to her blood stained garments.

She glances down. "What about them?"

"Take them off," I command, my tone brooking no argument.

I watch as Valeria hesitates, a look of defiance on her face as she clutches her hands against her chest. "No."

"They are soiled...with damning evidence. Take them off."

She stands tall, her face flushing with rage as a hot blush spreads from her cheeks to the tips of her ears. "What, like this?" she snaps.

Before I can react, she starts ripping off her clothes with both hands, sending bloody rags in my direction. Her wild eyes are daring and the curves of her body send a thrill down my spine. She moves with an animalistic grace that tells me even if I were to overpower her, she would never surrender without a fight. Mesmerized by the way her skin shimmered in the low light, I found myself wondering what it would feel like to have her underneath me, suppressed yet begging for mercy.

"Yes, like that." My voice is low, like a whisper.

Her eyes flash as she unleashes a torrent of obscenities, her voice hot with rage. I stand motionless, holding my tongue and taking each barb without flinching. I've already been called every single name in the book. None of the vulgarities she directs at me hurts me. And I know that soon enough she'll be begging for my sympathy.

But at this point, I'm done with her theatrics. Between the snitch Nigel and a lieutenant who stepped out of line for slapping a woman, I've had enough for one day.

I grab her waist and back her up against the wall, looming over her. I press my solid core against her soft curves. I'm so fucking hard, it hurts. A gasp escapes her lips when she feels it against her. Her smooth skin presses against me, and the only barrier between us is a pair of panties and bra. She trembles in anticipation, her shallow breaths causing her bare chest to rise and fall, and I feel the hard points of her nipples pushing against the fabric. The heat that emanates from her body is almost too much to bear.

I dip my head down to whisper in her ear, my lips brushing against the soft skin of her neck as I speak. "Settle down, little rabbit, you're making my dick hard."

Valeria's eyes are wide with surprise and fear but she doesn't protest or try to escape my grasp. *"Bastard."*

"That is accurate."

"What do you want?" she demands.

"You." It's quite simple, yet not so simple after all.

I wait for her to stop struggling because I am a patient man. She seems almost resigned to whatever punishment I have planned for her and this only fuels my desire more.

I can see the fear in her eyes, but it only adds to the thrill of the chase. I run my hands over her body, reveling in the way she shivers at my touch. She's mine now, and there's nothing she can do to resist me.

My fingers curl around the cold metal of the handgun, and her body trembles with fear. I see terror in her eyes as she desperately begs for mercy.

"Please, don't do this," she says.

"This is the gun you used to shoot my father," I told her, running the edge up along her bare thighs and hips.

Her breath cuts off in her throat. "He was trying to rape me. He was an animal! He raised you; you're an animal too. You're all animals!"

I grind my teeth together. I've become increasingly aggravated over people comparing me to my father.

"Trust me, little rabbit, you haven't seen the animal in me yet."

She trembles against me and my dick twitches. I grabbed my father's gun from the table, and with a trembling hand pressed the cold steel against her bare skin. I pulled her panties to the side, and she gasped as the barrel of the gun made contact with her clit. She writhed against the pressure, her body hot and slick beneath my touch. Her breath came in short gasps as she closed her eyes and moaned softly.

"Fucking hot," I groan. "I bet this pussy gets soaking wet when a dick fucks it."

I want to fuck her into submission so badly, I can't think straight. I don't just feel the tension radiating around us. I smell it. The sweet smell of her excited desire fills the air like intoxicating honey. Something else was there under the sweet. A metallic scent. The blood of that fucking asshole is still on her skin. It reminds me that there are people out there that want to kill her to seek revenge.

I step back, my heart pounding in my chest as I force my hand away from her. I grab the rough grip of my semi-automatic and shove it down the front of my pants.

"Get cleaned up. *All the blood*. You smell like another man," I bite out.

She shoves at me. "You fucking asshole." Then she rushes past me, putting several feet between us.

As I pick up her clothes from the floor, she yells, "Give me back my clothes."

But I know that she won't be needing them anymore.

"You can't run anywhere if you're naked," I add.

"*Ugh*," she pants out in aggravation.

With my back turned, I grin.

From this day forward, she belongs to me, and I'll make sure that she knows it.

"There's a shower to wash that scumbag's filth off your skin," I call over my shoulder. "Lesson number one: another man touches you...it gets them a bullet to the face."

I walk out of the room, leaving her there.

I can hear her yelling after me, but I don't care. She's mine now, and there's nothing she can do about it.

Thirteen

Valeria

Hours have passed since Dante left me alone in this lavish room, surrounded by opulence that feels suffocating instead of comforting. The silence is deafening, amplifying the inner conflict that churns within me. Doubt and fear gnaw at my insides, weaving a tangled web of uncertainty.

I try to distract myself, glancing around the room, taking in the extravagant decor, but it all feels hollow, a facade to mask the underlying darkness. My mind races with questions, each one intertwining with the next, fueling my anxiety. Is this a game to him? A twisted power play? Does he truly care about me, or am I just another piece in his dangerous world?

As time stretches on, doubt about his intentions for me creeps in, whispering poisonous thoughts in my ear. Did I misread his intentions? Was I foolish to let him take me alive so easily? The ache of uncertainty weighs heavily upon my chest.

And what the fuck is wrong with me? Why am I attracted to such a murderous rampaging lunatic? Why do I wish it was his fingers against my pussy instead of his gun?

A voice echoes, reminding me of the danger that lingers beneath his every changing personalities. I'm torn between the desire to be genuinely loved and wanted by someone —*anyone*—and the need to protect myself.

I find myself pacing the room, the silence punctuated by the sound of my own footsteps. Every passing minute feels like an eternity, stretching the chasm of uncertainty wider. What if he never comes back? What if he goes off and gets himself killed with his reckless self? What if I'm left to navigate this labyrinth alone?

The conflicting emotions within me wage a relentless battle. Hope flickers like a fragile flame, threatened by the gusts of doubt. I want to believe that he's not going to be abrasive like his father and that maybe I can fulfill the contract that my own father set out for me. But fear taints every optimistic thought.

In this moment of vulnerability, I'm forced to confront my own insecurities. Am I strong enough to handle the truth, whatever it may be? Can I trust my instincts when everything seems shrouded in shadows? I'm a mere pawn in a game I don't fully understand, and the stakes are higher than I could have ever imagined.

I want to understand it. And I'm going to understand it. Come hell or high water.

As I glance at the clock on the wall, my heart sinks. Hours have slipped away, and still, no sign of Dante. Or anyone.

The room feels colder, emptier. Tears threaten to spill, but I refuse to let them fall. A seed of doubt takes root, whispering that I may be alone in this unfamiliar territory, left to navigate the unknown. Maybe I should've taken my own advice; I should've left for Italy way before this. Years ago.

I stand in front of the bulletproof window, staring out into the distance. The moon is high. Other people are sleeping in their beds at this hour. My mind is racing, trying to figure out how to escape when it's possible for me to do so. I know it's useless, but I have to try.

Wrapped in a bath towel, I turn around to explore the room. The walls are shockingly bright, so much so that it throws me back for a moment. My eyes are drawn immediately to an orange chair on the far wall, which catches a ray of moonlight and reflects it across the floor like shining stars off of a polished mirror. Curled into one corner, my own reflection peers back at me. I'm a mess. I turn away.

Farther along, there is a deep red door with a rectangular window covered by an ocean-blue curtain. To the right there is another door, this one dark and embossed with ornate whorls of wood. My gaze was drawn to the dresser in the corner of the room. An ornate silver tray held a dozen different perfumes and colognes, each with their own unique scent and shimmering glass bottles. I remember seeing the same assortment four years ago in that other room–the one I was trying to forget. These bottles had a gold emblem affixed to it, and an "A" stood out more prominently than all other letters.

The door slams open and I jump. Dante stands in the doorway, his gaze slowly scanning my body from head to toe. I'm wearing nothing but a thin white towel, which clings to my damp skin. He leans against the doorframe, one hand up high and the other holding a gun down low. His eyebrow raises, a smirk playing on his lips as he stares at me.

I dive across the room, scrambling into a corner as fast as I could. My heart pounds in my chest as I press myself against the wall, trying to make myself as small as possible.

He doesn't move and then I realize that he's only taunting me.

"There's no way out, little rabbit so don't even look for one," he says, his voice even. He shoves his gun his pocket. "Even if you do get out, my dogs will chase you down like animals."

I curse under my breath. "Where are my clothes, you jackass? I want to go home."

"Don't expect release anytime soon," he replies, tossing a silk gown at me which I don't catch so it falls to the floor. "Pick it up, put it on, and come downstairs. The food is already waiting."

"I'd rather starve to death," I shout at him.

He swings around and steps closer to me, his eyes darkening. "You either come downstairs to the dining room or I'll escort you into the room where I watched my father bleed out."

He picks up the gown and hands it to me.

I swallow hard, the memory of that night coming back to me in flashes. I don't want to end up like his father, but I don't want to give in to him either. I snatch the gown from him and he doesn't even wait for me.

There's a maid waiting for me by the door. She has a pair of heels in her hand. "Are you ready, ma'am?"

"Give me a moment," I tell her, trying to hide my tears as I took the heels from her.

I walked over to the mirror, my tear-stained cheeks reflecting back at me. I wiped away the tears with a towel and slipped into the A-line silver gown. I inhaled deeply and admired my reflection in the full-length mirror. The dress fit like a glove, its hem stopping just above my knees. It is beautiful—I hadn't felt this confident in an outfit in a long time.

I smiled at my own courage as I remembered something my father had told me long ago: 'anyone can be bargained with, you just have to uncover their vice and exploit their virtue.'

I smiled at my reflection before turning around to face the open door. I knew exactly what I had to do.

Fourteen

Valeria

The dining room is filled with the scent of oak floors and walls of mosaic paintings. Its heavy wooden table stretches a dozen paces long, while the chairs are carved mahogany with dark red velvet cushions. A silver platter holding an olive loaf, wine-stained fingers, cheese and olives sits at the head of the table where Dante is seated. The crackling of embers in the fireplace holds its own against the sound of rain patting on the windows and roof. There is only one other chair besides his own, placed to the left of him.

He stands up and pulls out the chair. "Sit," he tells me, lowering his voice.

"I'm not a dog," I respond.

Seeing as how my show of defiance is getting attention from his house staff, I sit down and the tops of the platters are taken off of the food. My mouth waters at the rich, steaming scent of hot steak and lobster nestled next to a baked potato. The chilled wine has already been poured into glasses.

"Anything else, Mr. Argentieri?" one of his staff asks, their hands clasped behind their back and eyes focused on the floor.

"Just leave us." He waves his hand in a dismissive manner. The staff file out quickly, shutting the door softly behind us.

I sit at the table, eyeing the food spread out before me but make no move to take any, while Dante wastes no time in helping himself to the feast.

I sit in the chair, staring at the food on the table in front of me. I have not eaten a thing since lunch. I'm hungry but my stomach twists and turns with apprehension.

I can't shake the feeling that something is wrong with this picture. The room is so quiet that I can hear the sound of my own breath as I inhale deeply. Dante seems to be enjoying his meal, though, savoring each bite with relish.

He doesn't seem to care about his table manners at all. He eats with his mouth open and licks his fingers as he goes. I can't help but notice how sexy his lips look as he eats. I quickly push the thought out of my mind, disgusted with myself for even thinking it. It was so wrong that I should find such a lack of manners attractive, yet here I was, still thinking of it.

"What do you want from me?" I ask, breaking the silence.

"I told you already. I'm not going to repeat myself. I never do," he responds, his eyes flicking up to meet mine for a moment before he returns to his meal.

"Do you think I'm stupid? Do you really think I'm going to sit here and let you poison me?" I ask, my voice rising with anger.

"Suit yourself," he replies, unconcerned, pushing in a fork full of food.

"Why didn't you just take care of me when you found me? Put an end to this and sniper shoot me or something. What are you? A coward?" I taunt.

Dante hurriedly leaps out of his chair, sending the dishes and plates clattering to the floor. His eyes burn with intensity as he grabs me by the arm and hoists me onto the serving table. With an almost inhuman strength, he shoves aside the pastries that occupy the small table until there is nothing but a key lime pie. In one swift motion, he pushes the pie off the edge and it splatters on the cold floor. Every fiber of my being is alive with excitement as I can feel my heart pounding against my chest.

"You will watch your tongue," he warns.

"Or what? You will treat me like your father did?" I ask, my voice rising with anger.

"Don't taunt me, little rabbit," he says, his eyes blazing with anger. "You brought this on yourself."

"I'm a Cipriano, I don't do what anyone says."

In that moment, I know that I should have kept my mouth shut. I can see the dangerous look in his eyes, and I know that I've gone too far. I want to take back everything I've said, but it's too late. I've crossed a line, and I know that there will be consequences.

He moves closer, pushing himself between my legs and spreading them. His scent wraps around me like a blanket. The cologne he's wearing smells so good and it's becoming intoxicating.

His gaze is so intense that I can feel an almost magnetic attraction between us. His breath is hot on my neck as he leans in, and I find myself suddenly unable to move. The sexual tension between us escalates with every passing second until he softly grips my throat and then uses his calloused thumbs to caress the skin on my delicate throat.

"You don't break easily, do you?" he asks.

I don't know what to say. My tongue seems tied.

His fingers move up my body with agonizingly slow progress until his palm is caressing my breast through the delicate silk of my nightgown. I can't help but sigh softly in pleasure and lean into his hand, silently encouraging him to continue. The fabric feels slick beneath his thumb as he traces light circles around my nipple, which immediately hardens in response. A low whimper of pleasure escapes from me.

As his thumb and forefinger start to softly pull and twist, I clutch his shoulder blades tightly to help me keep from shaking. The intense pleasure of his fingers sends waves of electricity through me.

His fingers move up to my lips and he runs them across my mouth with an intensity that sends a shiver through me. I part my lips eagerly, inviting him inside, and he takes me up on the offer as his firm thumb slides past my teeth and caresses my tongue. His touch continues down my chin and when I think he's going to kiss me, he suddenly lifts my thighs and drags my dress all the way up to my waist. My skin burns in anticipation, knowing that my waxed pussy is completely exposed to him. I'm not wearing panties because he never bought any clean ones to my room.

A growl rumbles low in his throat as he looks down hungrily at my exposed pussy. His gaze darkens with an uncontrollable hunger. *"Fuck."*

As his hands travel down my exposed hips, I don't push him away. When he begins to stroke the sensitive folds between my legs, I can't help but arch my body towards him yearning for more contact. His fingers dip into my slick heat and start to move in and out slowly, giving me time to adjust as he adds another finger. He runs his thumb across my clit sending sparks of pleasure through me as it swells and grows harder from his caress.

I was swiftly losing the power of coherent thought. The sensation building inside me was unlike anything I had ever experienced before. It was more powerful than any physical pleasure I had managed to give myself. As it grew stronger, the warmth in my core became almost unbearable, but I found myself unable to stop or even slow down. I bit back a moan as my nails dug into the table's surface, leaving deep grooves in their wake.

Dante moves his skilled fingers in and out of me with practiced ease. His thumb teases my clitoris as his middle finger curls up, probing for my g-spot in a way that sends wave after wave of pleasure through my body.

"God! Fuck!" I throw back my head. "I'm going to..."

"Do it," he urges. *"Come for me."*

At his gentle urging, the emotions contained within me burst open. The sensation of pleasure condenses into a tight knot before expanding outwards, rippling through my body like a pebble hitting the surface of a lake. A sound between a moan and a cry leaves my lips as consecutive waves of pleasure surges through me.

Suddenly, he backs away and leaves me panting on top of the dessert table. He takes a seat back at the head of the table and starts cutting into his steak again as if nothing notable has happened.

What the hell has *actually* just happened? He's not going to say anything? *Do anything?*

I never get the chance to demand answers as someone raps hard against the double doors outside the dining room. The sound reverberates throughout the room and jolts me from my thoughts. To save myself any further embarrassment, I quickly hop off the table and straighten out my dress.

"Come in," Dante calls out tersely out over his shoulder.

The tall, imposing figure walks into the room with a confidence that commands attention. He is dressed in a sleek black suit that accentuates his broad shoulders, displaying an intimidating presence. His eyes quickly scan the area and lingers on me before walking over to Dante's table. He bends down to whisper in his ear. A spark of inquisitiveness flickers across Dante's face as he listens intently, and once the man finishes talking, Dante dabs at his mouth with a napkin and stands up.

The look on his face is unmistakable. Deep anguish and terror mixes in a disconcerting masquerade, warning me something is amiss. His eyes are distant, yet penetrating, as if he had heard something completely unexpected—something that disturbs him to the core.

Dante's gaze rests on me, and I can feel the intensity of his eyes from across the room. Just then a maid enters the room and he gives her an order in a stern voice, "Don't let her leave this room until she's eaten her food."

"*Si signore.*" The maid nods.

Two bulky bodyguards in dark suits hurry through the door, their presence like a gust of wind. The maid scurries out of their way as they post up against wall, probably there to make sure I don't try to escape. Without another word or glance in my direction, Dante turns on his heel and sweeps out of the room.

Fifteen

Dante

The warehouse is dimly lit, filled with crates and the stench of stale cigarette smoke. Every footstep I take reverberates through the empty space, a constant reminder of the danger that lurked in the shadows when I got here earlier.

Dead Moretti soldiers lay on the ground. Moretti is among them. His mouth and eyes is still gaped open as rigor mortis begins to set in. I didn't waste a bullet on him. I slit his throat when I got hold of him and made him look into my eyes as I watched him bleed out.

The sun is now rising, reminding me that I haven't slept in almost two days, but my work here isn't done.

Vito and I move cautiously, navigating the maze of crates, our senses heightened, and our guard never wavering. We've accomplished what we set out to do: taking down Moretti, the man who ordered the hit on me. A hit which failed. Yet, there's an unsettling feeling that lingers in the air, an unease that refuses to dissipate.

My mind is a tempest of thoughts and conflicting emotions. I know my father has enemies, but this sudden resurgence of rival mafia factions tests my patience and resolve.

As we scour the warehouse for any shreds of evidence, my eyes dart around, desperately searching for clues, for any connection that will unravel this intricate web of alliances and power struggles.

Vito's voice pierces the silence, laden with a mix of relief and concern. "We did it, Dante. That's at least one nutcase that won't be causing any trouble anymore."

Suddenly, I stub my toe on a metal box. I pull it out and slam it on a table. The lock pops off after one shot. I dump the documents out into the light. I scan them. "Look at this," I say to Vito, who comes over and leans over the papers. The air is hazy with dust as he shuffles through everything.

My jaw clenches, and my mind races to comprehend the gravity of what we've uncovered. Moretti's ties to another rival mafia faction suggests a much deeper entanglement, one that I thought my father had left behind way before his damning fate. It's as if the past, with all its vengeance and unresolved vendettas, has resurfaced, threatening to shatter the fragile peace I've painstakingly built.

"We might have gotten Moretti...," I reply, my voice tinged with exhaustion. "But this goes beyond him, Vito."

Vito nods, mirroring my concern with his own expression. "Seems like they want a piece of our action, boss. They're trying to shake things up. You've gotta show them you're here to stay. That you're not backing down without a fight if it comes to that."

"It will come to that. It already has," I say.

My mind drifts back to my father, the legendary figure in the Italian mafia world. The enemies he made...the grudges they must have against him. Just because I took over, doesn't mean they'll forget what an Argentieri did to them.

With each piece of evidence we uncover, my determination grows stronger. I realize that I cannot turn a blind eye to these challenges and hope they go away, because they won't. I must face them head-on, expose their plans, and safeguard everything I hold dear. The fire of vengeance burns within me still.

In the depths of my soul, I make a silent vow to protect the Argentieri empire, to untangle the mysteries that surround my father's enemies and unfinished business.

The path ahead is treacherous, fraught with danger and uncertainty, but my resolve remains unyielding. Each step I take brings me closer to the truth, closer to the inevitable clash that awaits me. And I've decided...I will face it head-on, with unrelenting determination.

Sixteen

Valeria

The evening sun casts its warm glow through the room, painting the walls with a soft, golden hue. I've spent the entire day confined within these four walls, isolated from the outside world. The luxurious furnishings, once a symbol of opulence, now serve as a constant reminder of my captivity. Time seems to stretch endlessly, the minutes merging into hours, each passing moment intensifying the knot of frustration and confusion within me.

The only respite from this suffocating solitude comes in the form of the kind-hearted maid who has so far brought me breakfast and lunch and distractions. Books, magazines, and a television serve as my companions, providing an escape from the stark reality of my situation. I find solace in their pages, losing myself in the fictional worlds crafted by the imaginations of others.

But as the hours crawl by, my mind wanders, consumed by questions and doubts. What is Dante's true intention? Why has he kept me locked away in this room, like a fragile bird in a gilded cage? Is he merely toying with me, or does he have genuine feelings hidden beneath his hardened exterior? The mixed signals he sends, the moments of tenderness followed by tense silence, leave me torn.

This can't have been worse than turning me into the actual police, but I know why he can't do that.

The maid, Sofia, only speaks highly of him, which leaves me even more confused. I recall my conversation with her about Dante.

As Sofia moves about the room, her presence a calming force amidst the chaos of my thoughts, I seize the opportunity to engage her in conversation. The questions that have plagued my mind demand answers, and Sofia, with her ten years of service to Dante and his family, might hold some insight.

My hands trailing along the cool surface of the dresser, I bent forward to take in the sweet, exotic aromas wafting from within the bottle. "What are these perfumes? Where do they come from?" I breathed softly, captivated.

"When Dante's mother was alive, she owned a business. She had her own fragrance line. It's still around today, but not as profitable now that she's not here to run it anymore," Sofia replies.

"Sofia, may I ask you something else?" I venture, my voice laced with a mix of curiosity and hesitation.

She looks up from her task, a warm smile gracing her lips. "Of course, dear. What's on your mind?"

I take a moment to gather my thoughts, unsure of where to begin. "Tell me about Dante. What kind of man is he, really?"

Sofia's eyes sparkle with a hint of nostalgia as she pauses, her hands stilling momentarily. "Dante... He's a complex man, Valeria. He has been through more than most can imagine, seen things that have shaped him into the person he is today."

I lean in, eager to absorb every word, hoping to catch a glimpse of the enigma that is Dante beneath the hardened exterior. "But is he...is he capable of kindness? Can he ever let his guard down?"

Sofia's expression softens, her voice carrying a gentle reassurance. "Oh, my dear, you have no idea. Dante may project strength and ruthlessness, but inside, he carries a heart burdened with pain and vulnerability. He's learned to protect himself, to wear a mask in this dangerous world. But

I've seen glimpses of another side of him, the tenderness he's capable of. Why do you think I stay?"

I shrug. "Maybe they pay well," I respond shyly.

Sofia laughs. "I'm paid more than some CEOs in this city, but that's not why I stick around."

Her words stir conflicting emotions within me. The realization that Dante's hardened persona may be a facade, a defense mechanism, fills me with a mix of hope and trepidation. Could there be more to him than meets the eye?

"I can't say the same about his father...although he tried," Sofia adds quietly and then gets up swiftly with the basket, heading for the door.

"What do you mean?"

She smiles meekly. "I've said enough about Dante. I'll say no more."

"Wait..." I swallow. Seeking guidance, I press further. "Is Dante capable of forgiveness?"

Sofia's gaze meets mine, her voice gentle but firm. "Valeria, accidents happen. I've seen Dante forgive before, if the apology is sincere. If he sees that you truly regret what happened, it might sway him. But know that trust is a fragile thing, my dear. It takes time to rebuild."

Her words offer a glimmer of hope, a possibility that redemption and forgiveness are not entirely out of reach. I cling to the idea that there might be a way to bridge the divide between us, to understand each other's pain and find common ground.

As Sofia continues her task, her movements graceful and purposeful, I reflect on her words. Perhaps, if I can find the courage to confront Dante with genuine remorse, if I can show him the depths of my regret and desire to make amends, there is a chance for redemption, for a future beyond the confines of this room.

The path ahead remains uncertain, but just maybe I can unravel the layers of Dante's guarded heart.

And now, as evening descends upon the mansion, casting long shadows across the room, my thoughts swirl in a whirlwind of emotions. I yearn for freedom, for the touch of the cool evening breeze against my skin, for the vibrant pulse of life outside these confining walls.

I miss riding through neighborhoods and looking for new homes on the market to show. I'm restless and I just want to do something other than lounge around. I once thought that no one would ever want to marry me. I wouldn't be a good house wife. I don't like staying in the house all the time.

Just as the despair threatens to overwhelm me, the door swings open without warning, and there Dante stands, the source of my torment and my fleeting moments of happiness. I don't know why but anger surges through me, fueled by his intrusion, by the lack of respect he shows for my personal space. Just barges in here after leaving late into the night last night and leaves me the entire day alone to myself. Beneath the fury, a glimmer of relief ignites. At least he hasn't completely forgotten me.

Dante's eyes meet mine, and I see a hint of remorse, a flicker of something resembling regret.

I think he might say something that would explain this craziness he's putting me through, but when he opens his mouth, he says, "It's time to have dinner."

The memory of his touch burns through my veins like fire, and I remember how he pinned me to the table, dominating my body with every thrust of his finger. The pleasure builds until it shatters my entire being, leaving me powerless under his command. He had used my body, bending it to his will.

His words hang in the air, devoid of any explanation, and frustration boils over, erupting in a scream that tears through the room. "Leave!"

His eyes narrow as if he doesn't understand my outburst.

I want to understand him, to grasp the motives behind his actions. But right now, all I can feel is the overwhelming need for him to respect my boundaries, to acknowledge that I'm not some fucking prisoner or slave or sex toy to play with.

As Dante stands there, his expression a blend of surprise and resignation, I realize the power rests within me. The power to demand respect, to assert my own desires and needs.

With a shaky breath, I muster the strength to hold his gaze, my voice steady but laced with defiance. "You think you can just bring me here and keep me like a lost pet."

As the room fills with charged silence, I await his response, my heart pounding in my chest, a mixture of fear and hope intertwining within me.

Dante stares at me, his expression unreadable. I'm not sure what he's thinking, and I don't know what to expect. Then, gradually, something shifts in his demeanor, and suddenly he is lifting me up and placing me onto the bed.

He grips my throat with one hand and leans down to kiss me with both intensity and passion. In that moment, all my doubts dissipate into nothingness as I relax into his embrace, wanting nothing more than for him to stay right here with me forever.

The kiss is explosive and mind-numbing, the sensation of his lips against mine like a hurricane of emotions. I taste my own desire in his mouth as he ravages me with a hunger that surpasses understanding. His hands wander down my body, igniting every nerve until I feel like I'm burning from the inside out. His touch is both gentle and demanding, as if he's claiming me for his own.

Suddenly I remember what happened the last time. He's toying with me. My heart is pounding inside my chest as I try to make sense of what's going on. He's going to continue taunting and toying with me. But why? Why would he do this to me? Is this some kind of weird game he wants to play before destroying me completely?

His mouth claims mine hungrily as one of his hands slides down between my legs. I back away from him, but he starts to unbuckle his belt. He's already hard as steel. I can tell from the way his dick imprints the pants.

I'm instantly aroused, thinking about how much more fulfilled I'd be if he had used his dick instead of his fingers last night. But no...I'm not just some sex toy for pleasure whenever he wants it.

I shakily reached my arm behind me and felt around the space beneath the pillow until I found the cool metal handle of the steak knife I had snuck upstairs after he abruptly left me at dinner a few nights prior. My fingers trembled as I grabbed it.

As he moves closer to me, I can feel the heat emanating from his body and sense the hardness of his arousal pressing through his pants.

I refuse to let my feelings get in the way freedom, and Dante Argentieri had no right to steal that away from me.

I thrust the knife upward with ferocious intensity. Dante moves fast, but his reflexes aren't quick enough: his palm collides with my weapon as he yanks it away and throws it on the floor. It slides across the floor and lands against the door with a thud.

When I meet his gaze this time, I know things are about to get ugly.

Dante's grip tightens around my throat and I feel a sudden rush of pleasure that starts in the tips of my toes and travels all the way up to my brain. Blood—*his blood, blood I spilled*—is draining from his palm down my neck and cleavage. I squirm under his touch, unable to understand why his slightest touch inflames me no matter how violent or what kind of mood he's in.

"You have a drive to kill in your blood," he growls.

I meet his gaze dead-on, my voice a menacing whisper. "I'm a Cipriano. We all do."

"Well, your daddy gave you away and guess what?" He leans down and whispers. "You're not a Cipriano anymore, little rabbit. You're mine now."

I let out a short laugh, my cheeks growing hot. "You won't be able to handle me."

His dark eyes meet mine, searching for something hidden in my gaze. I feel the tension rising between us, like sparks in the night air.

"Is that a challenge?" he finally asks.

"Yes." Once the word left my lips, I couldn't take it back.

He slides forward on his knees, positioning me in a seated position against the headboard. His breath whispers against my skin as he pulls away, the heat of him lingering like a whisper. He unhooks his belt with deliberate slowness and my heart begins to race in anticipation. The buckle clicks open; the sound feels like a gunshot in the silent room. When he reveals himself, I gasp at the size of his erection—it's thicker and longer than I'd imagined. Veins snake along the length of it, and the thick head slightly bends towards the left. He's at least nine inches long, almost as thick as my wrist.

"Have you ever sucked dick before?" he asks as he strokes his hard length.

"No." I lick my lips and my pussy clenches as a droplet of precum spills from his swollen tip.

"Open your fucking mouth," he commands.

I part my lips slowly.

"Suck," he growls.

I grip the base of his cock and open my mouth to lick off the pre-cum first. It's both sweet and salty, like an irresistible tease. Then, I take in the rest of his length. He begins thrusting, a slow then fast rhythm that hints at what it will feel like when he's inside me. If he's ever inside me...

I'm lost in the moment as I let instinct take over.

He grips my hair with both hands, and pulls me closer towards him so he can thrust harder against my tongue.

I take his plundering length into my mouth, feeling aroused once more and my nipples harden from the intensity of this act.

My insides burn when he moans and speaks fervently in Italian. His thrusts become more forceful, making me gag and choke. I recoil from his grasp, but he tightens his grip in my hair and pulls me back towards him. Tears are streaming down my face, yet he continues thrusting against my lips. A deep part of me desires this cruel domination and his roughness.

A guttural howl escapes his lips as his manhood grows taut; the rush of warmth comes with a sudden burst of cum shoots against the back of my throat.

The flavor is salty and grainy, as if packed with secrets. I sense a hidden sweetness as if it's meant to be savored like the aftertaste of a night of passion. It could be imagined as such; or maybe that's just me.

Before I have a chance to think about it any further, he grabs my face and tilts my chin up so I am still facing him as his throbbing dick stays lodged in my mouth with his cum now inside.

"Swallow it," he orders.

I do as he commands, savoring the aroma and taste that linger on my tongue. As I swallow, I can feel the warmth of the liquid spreading through my body; it's like a mark of ownership has just been placed on me, imbuing me with his essence.

He pulls out his cock and tucks it back into his boxers.

"Aren't you going to fuck me?" I ask, whipping my mouth with the back of my hand.

His tongue flicks out past his lips. "Have you ever been fucked?"

My heart jumps and I don't answer.

"Trust me, principessa, I'm going to fuck you until I ruin you for everyone else." He strokes the underside of me chin. "But not now. I'm going to make you beg for. Make you drop to your knees for it. And then...only then...will I fuck you like there's no tomorrow. Do you understand?"

I nod. A tremor runs through me. I can't help it.

The longing that was present in his gaze moments ago is now replaced with pure loathing. He despises the woman he believes I am. I can't forget now that I shot his father, and I definitely can't forget that I cut his palm. The blood evidence is all over us now.

I look downward. "I'm sorry," I whispered.

"You're not sorry, little rabbit. Neither am I for taking you like this. That's why you're going to pay until I've decided you're done paying." His voice is like a hammer coming down on an anvil, and I am afraid of the finality of it.

He backs away off the bed and stands to his feet. He extracts a white handkerchief from the inside of his of his blazer and wraps it tightly around the cut on his palm. "Sofia will bring dinner to your room tonight."

I watch him leave. As soon as the door shuts, I collapse onto the bed and let out a loud scream of distress.

My survival is merely a delay. All I've done is add some extra time on this earth before something bad happens.

But I don't think I'm going to make it through this situation in one piece.

Despite what I've just learned about him, I don't think he'll grant me that kind of mercy.

Seventeen

Valeria

After stepping out of the confines of my room, I'm breathing in the crisp air outside. The fresh scent of autumn leaves and burning fires is laced with a note of freedom and apprehension.

I think I can have some alone time for a moment, but then Sofia comes racing behind me in the back courtyard. She has probably just discovered that I let myself out of my room.

Sofia's concerned gaze follows me, her voice tinged with worry. "Valeria, Dante didn't you say you could—"

"I don't care what Dante says, Ms. Sofia," I reply quickly.

"Are you sure you don't want an escort? It's not safe to wander alone. This property is huge. You can get lost if you don't know your way around."

I know that she's concerned that I might run off on her watch.

"I won't go anywhere. I won't run. I won't go far," I say. "I promise."

"Well, okay..." She looks weary.

"I need some space, Sofia, even if it's just for a little while."

Her lips purse in a mix of understanding and concern, but she relents. "Alright, just be careful. And remember, Dante probably won't be pleased if he finds out you went too far. Just stay within the main gates."

I offer her a grateful smile, knowing that she only has my best interests at heart. "I'll be cautious, I promise."

As I wander the huge courtyard, the walls towering above me, I get a wave of freedom and defiance. The breeze blows across the grand archways, carrying with it the scent of roses in all shades of red and pink. They climb over each other like an intricate quilt on either side of the entrance. Candles twinkle off silver mirrors standing atop heavy pillars. My reflection is echoed infinitely in every angle, bounced off the stone walls. A light blue dress hugs my curves just right then flares out at my waist as I move forward.

My moment of peace shatters abruptly as a hulking man fills the doorway, and his size towers over me. I instantly recognize one of Dante's goons, sent to keep tabs on my every move.

He drills me with a menacing stare. His hands are clasped in front of him. "Little lady, you need to go back inside. Now." His tone is unwavering and final.

I square my shoulders, refusing to let his authority dictate my actions. "And why should I? I don't care what Dante says. It's a crime to keep people against their will."

"Murder and attempted murder are also crimes." He picks his teeth with a piece of twig or something and clasps his hands in front of him.

I frown, shaking my head. Everyone and their freaking uncle knows what I've done. I would've been better off in jail.

"It's for your safety as well, Miss Valeria. Please, trust me on this."

But trust is a fragile thing, one that I'm hesitant to give so freely. I turn away from the bodyguard and head back into the mansion.

As I wander through the vast corridors and unseen rooms, I hear music coming down the hallway. Rock music with a whole lot of bass. The beats intwine with clanging of metal, leading me downward to the mysterious basement level. Curiosity takes hold, propelling me forward despite the warning bells in my mind.

I step into the room and instantly my heart stops. Sweat glistens off of Dante's body as he moves through a relentless routine of punches, squats, and presses. Even though my presence is uninvited, he doesn't break his focus on the task at hand. He wears grey sweats and his dick print is one helluva sight. He's hot as fuck and I think he knows it. His body is fashioned after a Greek god. His face reveals nothing of the thoughts that are surely going through his mind—no sign of anger or even acknowledgement for me.

"No need to stand back there, Valeria. You're already down here where I asked you not to come, so come inside," he says over his shoulders putting some dumbbells back on a rack.

I approach the gleaming workout equipment, a mischievous glint in my eyes. I can't resist the temptation to taunt him, to challenge the boundaries he's set for me. To make him regret ever locking me up in his mafia castle. "So this is where you disappear to when you're not busy playing the ruthless mob boss?"

Dante's gaze meets mine, a flicker of amusement dancing in his eyes. "Something like that, Valeria. Although, I remember telling you the basement levels are off limits."

I bit my bottom lip and pretended to think. "Oh, now I remember. Oh yes, you did. Then what goes on down here?"

"What you might expect," he grumbles. His back is turned to me but I catch a glimpse of him checking me out in the mirror.

"Well, what does that mean?" I pick up a pair of nunchucks from a weight bench in the corner. I had never seen one. I thought they were illegal, just like drugs. And then I remember what Dante actually does for a living. I've been away from the mob life for too long, it seems, but the ways of made mafia men are coming back to me now.

"It means you shouldn't be down here."

I twirl the nunchucks in my hands, trying to hide my growing frustration. The weight of the weapon feels foreign, and the unease within me deepens. I watch Dante closely, his stern expression betraying nothing but a subtle hint of concern.

"But why won't you tell me, Dante?" I press, my voice tinged with a mix of defiance and curiosity. "I know who you are. I know what you are. I know about the things you do. What is it that you're hiding from me?"

Dante's jaw tightens, and he finally turns to face me, his gaze piercing through my defenses. There's a flicker of something in his eyes, a glimpse of the darkness that resides within him.

"Valeria, this world, my world, is not one of frivolity and ease. It's a life full of darkness and dread, as you well know," he says with a hint of regret. "But I can no longer deny you your place in it; You were born to be a mafia princess after all. Just be careful not to be taken down by its crossfire. And what you know...sometimes it can come back to haunt you."

I take a step forward, my grip on the nunchucks tightening involuntarily. "I don't want to be sheltered, Dante. I ran from your family for four years, but I can't run from my fate. If all I'll ever know is this life, I want to be ready."

Dante's features soften for a brief moment, but it's quickly replaced by a resolute determination. "Ready for what?"

"For war...if need be," I say quietly.

"Revenge doesn't suit you," he says quietly.

"You can seek revenge for your father, but I can't seek revenge for mine," I snap.

"You don't know what you're talking about." He reaches out, swiftly taking the nunchucks from my hands and placing them aside with a controlled motion.

My heart sinks, the weight of his words settling heavily upon me. It seems that the walls he's built around himself are impenetrable.

I blink. "I'll have to learn myself then, but if this is how it has to be at first, then I'll stay where you want me. Rewrite the contract. Use me as you want and then let me go. You can do it. You're the boss now. But don't think for a second that I'll stop questioning, that I'll stop seeking answers as to what happened to my family. You brought me back into this life. And now it's too late. You did that."

I attempt to turn away, but he catches my waist with one arm and pulls me to him. His lips are on mine before I can protest, and a warmth spreads through my body. He reaches behind me and when I look over his shoulder, I spot the rope in his hands. His grip tightens around my wrists before I can take a breath.

My eyes widen as I feel his strong hands wrap around my wrists. "What are you doing?" I ask.

He pulls me up towards the metal pole mounted high on the wall and swiftly ties my wrists to it. His lips graze my neck, sending chills down my spine and I feel the warmth of his breath against my ear as he whispers, "Making sure you don't try to fucking kill me."

He kneels before me, his hungry eyes roaming my body as my dress rides higher, revealing the soft curves of my thighs. I don't have panties. He won't allow me to have any. His fingers come alive on my skin, tracing a searing path up between my legs as his breathing grows more urgent. I can feel the heat radiating off his fingertips and the shivers of anticipation traveling through every nerve in my body.

"Have I ever told you how pretty your pussy is, principessa?" He whispers seductively, barely grazing the sensitive nub between my legs.

I'm trembling with need and he knows it. I feel completely overwhelmed by the pleasure coursing through my veins and I know he feels it too. My every nerve trembles with anticipation of what's to come.

A low whimper escapes me as I feel a pinch on my buttock.

"You have the sexiest ass I've ever seen," he says.

"Is that why you make me wear these revealing dresses?" I tease.

He groans and clamps down tightly, digging his fingers into the flesh of one of my ass cheeks and revealing the dripping wetness between my legs. My knees are weak. My toes barely touch the ground as he presses his wide shoulders under my thighs.

"You're soaking wet," he speaks, his voice a mix of scolding and desire. His lips brush against my jawline and the sensitive spot right behind my ear. "Do you want me to pound your tight pussy with my hard dick, Valeria? Spread your legs wide." His sultry command sends chills down my spine as his breath tickles my ear.

"Ohmygod," I pant.

He chuckles. "I don't think he's listening."

I feel a tingling sensation across my skin as my legs spread apart with no conscious instruction from me, allowing him to see the juices flowing from my aroused sex. His voice is deep and commanding: "Now put your legs over my shoulders."

I struggle against the restraints, my breath coming in ragged gasps as I whisper "I...I can't."

Dante's eyes darken with desire and he asks me, a sinister promise in his voice, "Do you want my tongue?"

A moment of desperation passes before I raise my body using every last ounce of strength, tiptoeing and leveraging against the restraints on my wrists. With trembling limbs I lift my legs over his shoulders, surrendering myself to him.

"Now that's more like it." He purrs into me like a feral animal, each syllable a thunderbolt that ignites the fire within.

His fingertips caress my wetness, back and forth. Two thick digits thrust into me, filling my tightness, and I can't stifle the moans that escape my lips. The mere thoughts running through my head are enough to bring me so close to climaxing. It won't take much more to push me over the edge.

His fingers move faster and deeper inside me, each stroke hitting that sweet spot that made my eyes flutter and my head swim with pleasure. His thumb caresses my clit lightly, almost too light to feel.

I writhe on his fingers, pressing my body into them as I thrust wildly. He adds another big finger to my tight entrance, the sensation overwhelming and nearly unbearable. I plead with him for release. He won't give me my freedom; at least he can grant me this.

A hot wave of pleasure crashed through him when he asks, "When you're fucking dick, are you always this hot?" His skin is scorching as he waits for my answer.

My silence only seems to turn up the heat even more. He slides his fingers into my wet sex, pushing and pulling steadily and expertly. My inside walls are trembling with pleasure as I take him in deeper, making explicit noises as his thick digits massage my inner depths.

"You're so tight, Valeria," he growled. He grabs me and spins me around, his blue eyes searing into mine. "When was the last time you fucked?"

"I-I haven't," I stammer, unable to take my eyes off him.

His lips stretch into a wicked grin. "You're a...ah, fuck. Do you know how much that turns me on? To know that you're untouched. *All mine to ruin.*"

"Then do it. Ruin me," I taunt, licking my lips.

With one swift movement he pins me against the wall, and I knew his pleasure had no bounds. He licks my pussy, sliding his tongue through the thick juices and moaning as he eats. His hands slides up my inner thighs, teasing my skin before finding the most sensitive spot. He circles it slowly, not too fast nor too slow, just right.

"You taste like honey," he moans into my pussy. "So sweet. So wet."

I'm so close to orgasm; I can feel it coming on. I gasp in pleasure as he shifts his lips downward and lightly brushes his teeth over me. He moves back up and teases me with long, hard licks before sucking on my clit. It feels like pure bliss as I ride wave after wave of pleasure until I'm trembling from head to toe in ecstasy.

"I bet you want to fuck a hard dick right now, Valeria."

"Yes. Please..."

"Never be so quick to lose what you can't get back."

He's driving me crazy and I feel like I'm going to explode all over his tongue any minute.

He reaches up and his hands slide over to my breasts, kneading them before teasing my nipples with light touches and soft kisses that drive me wild with desire. He slides his fingers down to my core again and rubs gently while pressing his thumb against my clit in a steady rhythm that's driving me insane.

My walls quiver and ripple around his tongue as he fucks me with it and I let out an uncontrollable moan just before reaching climax. Every muscle tightens and contracts around him as I come undone in pleasure.

He sucks my clit until the last throes of pleasure have passed. My vision was cloudy, my breath heavy and ragged as I felt his hands untying my wrists. My arms fell like stringless marionettes to my side and I instinctively leaned in towards him, aching for a touch. I think he's going to fuck me. Give me the night of my life, but then he takes two steps back. His lips curl into a mischievous grin as he steps away from me, pointing to the door. *"Leave."*

Shock and confusion runs right through me. *"What the fuck?"*

He spins on his heel and strides away, his arrogance apparent in the stiffness of his shoulders. He lays himself face up on a bench and begins to lift weights, his eyes fixed upward and pointedly avoiding mine. But I see it anyway: the huge bulge pressed against his grey sweatpants, an unmistakable indication of arousal. He is as hard as a brick. Yet he won't fuck me.

My rage at Dante's actions is boiling up inside me, and I want to scream. I spin around and race out of the exercise room, barely able to contain my frustration as I slam the door shut behind me.

Eighteen

Valeria

I've been purposefully avoiding Dante. For almost two days now. He knows why. He's taunting me. Playing me like a pawn on a chessboard.

I'm standing in the middle of my new bedroom, staring out of the window at the landscapes placing new flowers in the already beautiful bed in the courtyard, when Sofia knocks on the door. *"Signora Valeria,"* she says in her thick accent, *"Il signor Dante è dovuto partire stamattina per lavoro. Se hai bisogno di qualcosa, devi farmelo sapere."*

My heart sinks at the news. Dante left on business early this morning. He won't be back for a few days. What the fuck?

She continues telling me he has allow me free reign of the first and third floors, a small separate gym next to the pool, and the courtyard. *"Inoltre si può avere libero accesso solo al terzo e primo piano e al cortile e ad una piccola palestra, ma restando entro i cancelli della residenza."*

"Grazie, Miss Sofia." I sigh and she leaves me alone.

Dante left me alone in this mansion. He may have promised me free reign in limited areas, but what's the point of that if I have no purpose here? What exactly did he want besides to drive me insane for murdering his rapist father?

I need to get back to work or I'll be fired. The thought of losing my job that I actually like, my purpose, my independence, is unbearable. Everyone probably thinks I flew out to Italy, but my planned vacation—which I haven't even taken yet—will be over soon. People will wonder and start looking for me. Someone will probably even call the cops. The landlords will evict me from my condo without hesitation and my car will be repossessed.

Suddenly, the door opens again and in walks one of Dante's men. I recognize him from the day we were at the home for sale. He was the one with the briefcase. He must've been some kind of finance person or accountant. Someone who handles the legal work or money for the Argentieri family.

He pauses in the doorway. "You don't know me by name yet, Signora Valeria. You can call me Scottie. I've come to tell you that we've secured the property in the areas you are free to roam," he says, and then places a small black card on the dresser. "And to leave you this. You may order clothes or whatever you need and have it delivered to the address taped on the back of the card." Then he turns to leave.

Before he can take another step, I speak up. "I'm going to lose my job if they don't know where I am," I say, the desperation clear in my voice. "I need a phone to let them know I've been kidnapped by a psychotic mob boss." He laughs but doesn't argue with me. He knows it's true.

"Don't worry about your job, Signora Valeria," he says smoothly. "Dante now owns the entire real estate firm, and I can assure you that your checks will still arrive."

"My car—"

"—has been warehoused. Your rent has been paid through the year."

I'm flabbergasted. Dante now owns the entire firm? How is that even possible? And why didn't he tell me? The creep knows just what to do so others won't bother to come look for me.

Men like him think they can just own the world by just buying everyone out. There would come a time when that strategy would fail.

I can feel anger bubbling up inside me. How dare he leave me here without any explanation, without any purpose, without any control over my day? I may as well have been in a prison serving time for the murder I committed. This wasn't even the mafia way. My father would've had a person who did what I did killed on sight.

I can't wait to see Dante again so I can give him a piece of my mind. Fucking womanizing playboy bastard!

But at the same time, I can't deny the other feeling that's been gnawing at me since I first laid eyes on Dante: attraction. It disturbs me to feel this way, to be drawn to a man who is so controlling, so manipulative, so...dangerous.

I shake my head, trying to clear my thoughts. I need to focus on finding a way out of this situation, of this country, of this...situation. I'm still a player in the game; I just haven't utilized all my moves yet.

Nineteen

Dante

I step out of the car, my eyes frantically scanning the empty street for any sign of danger. Vito follows close behind me, his fingers already wrapping around the handle of his gun in anticipation.

We've ventured to an unfamiliar part of town on a desperate call from an old acquaintance, Rick Johnson—accused of embezzlement by the feds.

He swears he's been framed and promises his loyalties and resources if we could help him uncover who leaked his involvement to the cops. He believes someone connected to my network is behind it. Despite the ambiguity, I am determined to listen to what he has to say.

Vito and I take cautious steps into the eerily quiet building. We can see no security guards, no cameras; it's almost as if we are expected. We make our way to the partner's office and when we arrive, his wife is already there waiting for us.

"Where's your husband?" I ask her.

"I don't know," she says, wringing her hands. "I'm the one who called you about him going missing. He disappeared a few days ago. He left behind a trail of unpaid debts and angry mobsters. They've been threatening me and my family. I didn't know who else to turn to but I know that he trusts you, Mr. Argentieri."

I look at Vito, and we both know that this isn't good. We have a lot of money tied up in this guy, and now he's vanished without a trace. It doesn't make any sense.

"We need to find him," I say to Vito.

A feeling—a sense of dread—twists in the pit of my stomach. Something strange is happening here, and I have a feeling it isn't going to be good.

We start searching his office for clues, anything that might lead us to where he is or what has happened to him. After ten minutes of searching, we find a laptop revealing a hidden compartment filled with USBs and documents which seem to have a stamp of a nighthawk on it. I've seen the symbol before somewhere.

Before we can investigate further, Vito grabs my arm in alarm as he notices someone outside looking towards us. It's time to go before they find out who we are and what we're up too.

"Send a team down there. Track them," I say.

Vito flips out his phone. "Pay attention at five o clock. Tail him. Detain him for questioning, and take care of him if necessary."

We hurriedly made our way out of the building, hoping that the documents would take us somewhere.

As we cautiously make our way out of the building, a savage attack takes us by surprise. We duck for cover as they shower us with bullets, our attackers' necks marked with nighthawk symbol tattoos. Raucous shouts and piercing screams fill the air as Vito and I dodge the bullets. Vito and I retaliate in kind, picking them off one by one while taking out anyone who stands in our way. There's no time to think—my heart is pounding, my senses heightened as the adrenaline courses through my veins. This is what I'm made for, this fight-or-die moment when skill and reflexes are all that stands between life and death. My driver pulls up to the curb and we dive in just as a wave of bullets misses their mark.

I'm one madman who doesn't like surprises. Rage surges through my veins like a river of fire as I bark out in frustration. My fist slams against the back of the seat in an eruption of fury that sends shockwaves throughout the car. The force of my anger makes me tremble, and I can feel heat radiating from every pore.

"We need to find out who's behind this," Vito says, his voice low and serious.

"I'm gonna find them and I'm gonna find Rick Johnson. Someone's going to pay."

Twenty

Dante

I walk into the luxurious mansion, my footsteps echoing in the grand foyer. As I make my way through the hallway, I catch a glimpse of Valeria sitting alone in the living room. Her back is turned to me, engrossed in a home decorating magazine. I can tell she's aware of my presence, yet she refuses to acknowledge me. Despite that, I can't help but be captivated by her beauty, even from this distance.

"Valeria," I call out, breaking the silence that hangs in the room. She takes a moment before turning around, and in that split second, I see something in her eyes that I've never witnessed before. Both hatred and longing.

She says nothing, only stares up and down the length of my body as if looking for injuries. It's like she knows. No matter. I'm not the type of man to whine about how I got shot and had to recover. She will never see that side of me. I suffer in silence. Always have. Always will.

"I'm back, Valeria," I announce, my voice steady yet tinged with a touch of weariness.

Her question follows swiftly, filled with an undertone of irritation, "Where have you been all this time?"

"On business," I respond, keeping my reply simple and matter-of-fact.

"Why?" Her snap echoes through the room, and I can sense her frustration building.

"I am a businessman. I take care of business," I state firmly, knowing that I don't owe her a detailed explanation. She knows the life we're both entangled in, she understands its demands and sacrifices.

Valeria's agitation intensifies, her words laced with frustration and desperation. "You've got some nerve. Making me your prisoner and then leaving here for days! My job is on the line—"

I interrupt her, cutting off her anxious ramblings, "Your job is not on the line, Valeria. I can assure you of that. I'll have your laptop brought to you tomorrow. You can work, if you'd like." My voice carries a note of reassurance, attempting to ease her worries.

She huffs in exasperation, her next words dripping with defiance, "I don't want to stay here all day, every day. I want to go places. You can't keep me here forever like I'm some fragile bitch. At least if I had been arrested for what I did to your father, I would have an excuse...and my freedom because of that excuse. You know what he was trying to do to me. He was going to rape me. You walked in and saw it all. You know I killed him in self defense. That's why you spare me."

Her statement hits me like a bolt of lightning, and a surge of conflicting emotions courses through me. But she's right. My father is an abusive animal. I remember vividly the events that unfolded, the choices she made, and the consequences that followed. There's a part of me that sympathizes with her, that understands the pain and fear she must have experienced. She was young then; we both were.

But I can't let that cloud my judgment. I walk towards her, closing the distance between us. She backs up.

"Don't walk away from me," I implore, my voice a mix of vulnerability and determination. Deep down, I crave her understanding, her acceptance, but I also know the complexities that come with our intertwined lives.

Valeria's eyes meet mine for a fleeting moment, a storm of emotions reflecting within them, before she turns away and continues on her path out of the living room. The tension hangs heavy in the air, and as she walks off, my gaze lingers on her retreating figure, a whirlwind of thoughts and feelings swirling within me.

At the doorway, she pauses and looks back. In that moment, I know she wants me to come after her. But I don't.

Twenty-One

Valeria

I wrap my silk robe around me, the cool fabric gliding against my skin as I make my way downstairs. I can't sleep. I guess the way I greeted Dante when he got back from his business trip is bothering me. It's late, nearing midnight, and the mansion is enveloped in a peaceful silence. A soft sigh escapes my lips as I descend the stairs, my thoughts consumed by the events of the past weeks.

As I reach the bottom of the staircase, I decide to grab a bottle of wine from the cellar. The dimly lit hallway casts an ethereal glow, and I make my way towards the wine cellar, my footsteps muffled by the plush carpet beneath my feet.

Aside for some off limits area, I had taken a tour of the Argentieri mansion by myself while Dante was away, so I know where mostly everything is. The home is quiet now, but I know for a fact that there are some overnight guards and security roaming around somewhere.

I feel the heft of the bottle in my hand and climb the staircase back to my room. As I reach the landing, a soft, inviting glow seeps from beneath a door which stands slightly ajar. The alluring light invites me closer and curiosity thrums through me like an invisible force, urging me forward.

Setting the bottle on a nearby table, I approach the open door with slow, careful steps. Peering inside, I see Dante, seated at an elegant oak desk, his back turned to the door. The room is bathed in the soft glow of a lamp, the warm light casting shadows on the walls. The gray stone of the fireplace, carved in intricate patterns and graced with delicate vines and flowers, is clearly visible behind him. A large canvas leans against one wall, carefully draped so as not to damage the paint.

I slip inside the room. "Dante?" I call out softly.

He doesn't respond, move, or flinch. His attention remains fixed on the night sky outside, lost in contemplation. He has a breathtaking view that captivates my attention too. The city lights twinkle in the distance, blending with the twinkling stars above.

The wooden floorboards creak underfoot as I advance towards Dante. The flickering candles on either side of him casts shadows across his sharp features, making it hard to read his expression. I came around the edge of the hard oak and stand before him, my heart racing as his eyes met mine.

For a moment, the world around us fades into insignificance. His eyes hold an intensity I can't quite decipher—a blend of infatuation and apprehension.

"Would you like some company?" I ask softly.

A spark of surprise lit up in his eyes. He says nothing, only reaches out and takes one of my hands. His calloused fingers feel gentle against my palms.

In that silent exchange, the unspoken emotions hang in the air, intertwining our fates. The weight of our connection, the depths of our shared secrets, weave an intricate web that binds us together.

As the seconds tick by, I find myself lost in the labyrinth of his eyes, my own inner conflicts swirling within me. I wonder what lies beneath the surface of this complex man, what demons and desires he battles within himself.

But for now, in this fleeting moment, all that matters is the pronounced electricity between us. The untold stories that bind us, the unspoken yearning that hangs in the air.

"Have you been working all night?" I ask.

"Not all night. I was just about to turn in for the night," he says.

"Do you ever have any fun, Dante? What do you like to do? As in...not killing," I ask.

He looks up without emotion and answers flatly. "Killing cowards, snitches, and double-crossers is fun."

I roll my eyes and groan. "Or as in...while you're not doing work to relieve stress."

"Yes. I do lot's of things to release tension after work."

"Do you need help now?" I ask quietly. "To relieve the tension."

My inquiry draws a faint smile as he leans back in his chair. "What do you have in mind?"

I step closer to him, moving between his legs. His broad shoulders and muscular arms are tense with stress, yet I can sense the hidden desire simmering beneath.

"Something I think you will like a whole lot," I reply, licking my lips.

The suggestion hangs in the air between us. Without another word, I pushed down the straps of my gown and it lands in a heap at our feet. My skin feels as if it was ablaze beneath his gaze and a hot breath escapes his lips in a gasp of awe.

I drop to my knees on the floor in front of him, my eyes lowered in submission. I tremble as I reach out and lightly graze his belt buckle with my fingertips.

"Valeria," he breathed, his voice a tender whisper as he encircles my wrist with his strong grip. His fingers curled around mine.

"This is what you wanted. You wanted me to submit," I whisper, barely audible. "Well, here I am."

His eyes smolder as he reclines and unzips his boxers, revealing his stiffening erection. His thick member juts out, standing proud like a work of art. His breath catches in anticipation as I lower my head and lick up and down the length of it. My saliva slickens the surface before I take him tightly in my hand and begin to pump up and down with pleasure, feeling each vein protruding beneath my fingers.

My God," he groans, his breathing becoming more and more labored as I continue to pleasure him. His grip tightens on my wrist, and I can feel the pulse of desire radiating through his veins. Each stroke sends electric pleasure coursing through my body, my own arousal growing with each passing second.

"God isn't here," I tease, casting my eyes up at him as I lick around the base of his dick. His eyes darken in response, the flames of passion burning brighter with each movement of my tongue.

I take him fully into my mouth, relishing in the salty taste or his skin and savoring every single drop of pleasure that courses through me. His hand moves from my wrist to tangle itself in my hair as I roll it around in an effort to increase the intensity for him.

"You're fucking sexy," he pants, his fingers tugging gently at strands of hair as he thrusts further and further into my welcoming mouth. His hips arch off the chair as he explodes with pleasure, his essence spilling down the back of my throat. As he holds my head down to take all of his cum, I gag on his thick semen.

I do my best to swallow all the cum pouring out of Dante's dick, though some escapes and slides down my chin before dripping onto his swollen testicles. Once he finishes, he releases his grip on my head, letting me come up for air. I take a few deep breaths, trying to slow down my heart rate that had been racing during the act.

He stands from the chair and grabs his semi-erect dick and presses the tip against my lips. "Lick up what you've missed. Every drop." His hand tangles in my hair, forcing my head back down to his twitching dick.

My mouth hungrily wraps around him, devouring every inch of his stiff member. I lick and suck with a fervor that drives him wild, my tongue spiraling up and down the length of him until I can hear his breathing grow more rapid in anticipation. With every moan he releases my hunger intensifies, sending tingles down my spine as I pleasure him.

I use my tongue to trace a circle around his testicles, delicately licking them. I then skirt along the base of his shaft, tasting every bit that has seeped out. My tongue wraps itself around him as I glide up from root to tip, and when I reach the head, I let my tongue linger over his slit, picking up any drops that remain.

As I'm working his dick, he's taking off his clothes. He grabs the back of my head, controlling the pace. His hips thrust uncontrollably, pushing him deeper and deeper into my mouth until I'm filled with intense pleasure that radiates out from every inch of my being. With each frenzied movement, his shaft grows harder and tighter, until I'm forced to swallow nearly the entirety of his manhood again.

Out of the corner of my eyes, I see him reach into his drawer and pull out a foil packet. After a string of curses and deep plunges down my throat, he bites out, "I can't use this with you. *Fuck it.*" He throws the condom back into the desk drawer.

His abrupt withdrawal from my mouth makes me cry out in anguish. H leads me to stand and tightens his grip on my throat and slams me back against the unyielding glass of the windows—the same ones he had been silently gazing through moments ago. My lungs constrict as I fight for breath and my eyes burn with passion.

His lips crash against mine in a punishing kiss. I can feel the salty residue of his cum on my tongue. I know he can taste it too.

He pushes me, my spine crashing against the thin glass barrier that stands between us and the abyss below. My breath catches in my throat as he takes my hands and wraps my legs around him, pressing me closer to the fragile window. I feel like it's just one wrong move away from shattering beneath us; and yet I can't look away, feeling the thrill of a thousand feet deep with nothing protecting us from the fall. The view below is breathtakingly clear and inviting though. The clarity of my vision brings an illusion of standing on the edge with no boundaries, our bodies suspended within a void.

When I sneak a glance at him, my face is surely frozen with fear. His low voice shakes me as he rumbles, "Are you afraid of falling?"

I can only manage to give a small nod in response before burying my face against his chest. "Dante, please..." My heart thuds in my ears like thunder.

"Don't worry, little rabbit," he soothes me. "I will never let you fall."

He savagely thrusts his rigid and bulging manhood deep inside me, tearing through my maidenhead and triggering a skyrocket of sensations of passion, bliss, and pain. I struggle to keep myself from falling apart in sheer pleasure as he fills me completely, stretching me with his thickness. His powerful movements send shockwaves of delight coursing through my entire body as my tight sheath quivers around him. His urgent need radiates off him in heated waves and I gasp for air as ecstatic cries escape my lips. This is the moment of no return.

My tight walls cling onto him like a glove, and I feel my core dripping with desire. His entire body shudders with passion as he rocks back and forth inside me, each stroke bringing me deeper into pure bliss. With every thrust I feel myself being torn apart by his formidable might, and I gasp sharply from the overwhelming sensation of pleasure. Tears stained my cheeks as his velocity increases, taking me closer to an incomparable climax.

Dante's hot lips claim mine in an electrifying embrace. When our lips part, his dark eyes burn right through me with unbridled desire. A tide of intense heat spreads across his skin as his longing spills out of his body into mine. My gaze travels down from his face, tracing the curves of his chest as it throbs beneath the intensity of our kiss.

His arms grip me like iron bands as his deep voice reverberates in my ear. His full, passionate lips press against mine, sending a spark of electricity through my body. I'm surrounded by his warmth and strength, feeling safe and euphoric. His gaze pierces into me with profound emotion, so intense that I could never look away. The glass is slippery from all the sweat. I cling to him like my life depends on it.

"I've got you," he murmurs.

He stumbles back into the chair, taking me with him. His breathing is ragged and labored as I cling to him, feeling the warmth of his chest against my skin. The only sounds that fill the room are the ticking of the clock and our combined respirations, heavy and urgent.

He tenderly strokes my hair as his breathing evens out. Then he speaks softly, a single statement that resonates in my ears: "I like to sail."

My lips involuntarily curl into a smile against his chest, though I'm sure he feels it or senses it at least. There's something deeply hidden inside of him that I long to know but I know it won't be easy given his need for secrecy. I know it's going to take time. But...I think we have time.

Twenty-Two

Valeria

I step onto the sleek and luxurious private yacht, feeling a mix of excitement and curiosity as Dante leads me to the open deck. The sun casts a golden glow on the water, its shimmering waves captivating my attention. I can't help but admire the grandeur of the yacht, a testament to Dante's success and influence.

As we settle into the soft leather chairs, I breathe deeply, savoring the fresh clean air. The yacht begins to glide through the water and its gentle motion is soothing and serene. Turning my gaze towards Dante, I find him looking at me with a slight smile playing on his lips.

Our time last night was explosive. I mean, how many women can say they lost their V-card up against a glass window?

The gentle sway of the yacht beneath my feet brings a soothing rhythm to my thoughts as I stand on the deck, gazing out at the vast expanse of the sea. The wind tousles my hair, and the scent of the water fills my senses, carrying with it a sense of freedom and possibility.

Dante stands beside me, his gaze fixed on the horizon, lost in his own contemplation. I find myself yearning to delve deeper into the layers that make up this enigmatic man.

"Dante," I break the silence, my voice carrying a soft vulnerability. "Can I ask you something?"

He turns his attention towards me, his eyes a shade darker under the fading light of the sun hidden by clouds. "Of course, Valeria. You can ask me anything. If I can answer, I will."

I take a deep breath, gathering the courage to delve into the depths of our shared past. "We've both lost our mothers at a young age. It's a pain that shapes us, defines us in some way."

He swallows visibly. "I wish she were here still. I wish she had gotten better like she said she would."

"What happened, if you don't mind me asking?" I murmur, knowing my inquiry would likely set the tone for an upsetting conversation. I feel confused by Dante's behavior and questions were the only way to make sense of it all.

"She was addicted to my father's product," he states flatly. "Overdosed."

"I'm so sorry," I say softly. "Your...father must have been devastated."

"He wasn't," Dante replies coldly. "She wasn't a very good mother. He knew it. And I knew it. She slept with most of his bodyguards—all the ones that liked to play with fire. He was happy when she died—happier than I had ever seen him before."

"Oh..." I sigh, feeling a wave of sadness wash over me. "Well, my mom was sick too. Complications from a rare immune disorder kept her bedridden for months at a time. We expected it but...it was still rough. My father loved her though—he just had to move on with his life eventually. He wanted a male heir. He got it...and then he lost it and everything else. So now you know why including me in that deal with your father was like giving away...nothing."

"You aren't nothing," Dante said firmly. "And sometimes life hands us lemons."

"Did you ever imagine a different life for yourself? Something outside of the world we find ourselves in now?"

A flicker of nostalgia passes through his eyes, a trace of a wistful smile playing at the corners of his lips. "When I was younger, I used to dream of being a private investigator. Solving mysteries, uncovering the truth. It seemed like an escape, a way to seek justice for those who couldn't find it themselves."

His admission takes me by surprise, and a genuine smile tugs at the corners of my own lips. "A private investigator? I can picture you in a trench coat, navigating the shadows, unearthing secrets. Like Inspector Gadget." I giggle.

Dante chuckles softly, the sound bringing a warmth to my heart. "What about you, Valeria? Was there something you dreamt of beyond the confines of our world?"

I glance out at the endless stretch of the lake, my thoughts drifting back to the dreams I had long held within me. "I've always had a passion for entrepreneurship. Building something from the ground up, creating a legacy that goes beyond the boundaries of the life we were born into. I wanted to prove that I could thrive on my own, that I could make a mark in the world through my own abilities. And I lost so much time."

Dante's gaze lingers on me, a mixture of admiration and understanding. "You were only fourteen when you fled from our mansion. How did you manage?"

I smile. "I had help. Well, I asked for it mostly. I mean, I come from crime, so I know how to seek out fake IDs and counterfeits and stuff like that, so that's what I did. I lied a lot, but I made sure I never took advantage of anyone. I always gave back what I took."

"Ah, you're a survivor."

I nodd. "I am."

A gentle breeze brushes against my cheek, and I turn to face him fully, captivated by the vulnerability in his eyes. "Dante, sometimes I wonder if there's still a chance for us to pursue those dreams. To carve out a future that isn't bound by the weight of our past and the choices we've made."

His voice is soft, his words tinged with a mixture of hope and resignation. "Maybe."

I nod, a sense of peace settling within me. We may be caught in the intricate web of our lives, but here, in this moment, we can embrace the echoes of our dreams and find solace in the shared understanding of our pasts.

We had sailed for a couple hours past the docks of the city, out into open water until the captain steered us to a private shoreline. We had disembarked onto fifty lush acres of land, dotted with trees and wild grasses, leading up to a two-story lake house that seemed to be taken straight out of a dream. The property which sits on fifty acres is the perfect place to find solace from the busy city or take a much needed timeout from the world.

The sun radiates its warmth in the sky, painting an orange and pink glow on the horizon. We settle onto a picnic blanket nestled between tall trees with a wicker basket between us. An assortment of sandwiches, cheeses, fruits, and pastries adorn our plates while birds hum their melodies overhead. We swap stories from the past and muse about dreams for the future; time pauses around us, leaving only us in this secret moment.

After our meal, a car whisks us away to a high-end designer outlet mall. I stroll through the bustling outlet mall, shop windows displaying an array of tempting merchandise. Dante trails behind me, his presence both comforting and slightly unnerving. The bodyguards keep a discreet distance, their watchful eyes scanning the surroundings for any potential threats.

As I meander from shop to shop, my eyes catch a glimmer of crimson in a jewelry store. A stunning ruby necklace adorns a display, its vibrant hues beckoning me closer. Curiosity piqued, I step inside, the tinkling of the bell announcing my arrival.

The shop owner, a friendly-faced woman with sparkling eyes, greets me warmly. She recognizes my intrigue and kindly offers to let me try on the necklace. With a hint of anticipation, I accept her invitation, allowing the precious gem to rest against my collarbone. It's a breathtaking piece, exquisite in its craftsmanship, but I can already feel the weight of its price tag. After four years of living on budget, I finally know what it feels like to find value in things that money can't buy.

"Do you like it?" the shop owner inquires, a hopeful smile playing on her lips.

I catch Dante's gaze lingering on me, his eyes filled with amusement and adoration. It's a perplexing mix of emotions that sets my mind spinning.

"It's beautiful," I reply, my voice betraying a hint of longing. "But it might be a little too extravagant for me. Maybe later."

The shop owner's understanding gaze meets mine, and she nods empathetically. "I completely understand, my dear. How about something more modest? We have lovely bracelets that might catch your eye."

Relieved, I glance at the array of bracelets on display. My eyes settle on one delicate piece, adorned with intricate silverwork and a single sparkling stone. It's a symbol of elegance, a touch of luxury that I can accept without feeling overwhelmed. I point to it, a smile playing on my lips. "I'll take that one, please."

With the bracelet carefully wrapped and secured around my wrist, Dante and I continue our shopping adventure. We step into a designer clothing boutique, racks filled with exquisite garments and the promise of elevated style. I browse through the racks, running my fingers over fabrics and admiring the meticulous craftsmanship.

Dante's presence looms nearby, his presence a constant reminder that I am not alone. I feel so happy for once that I have someone to share secret smiles with.

The store attendant points me to a dressing room with all my garments. "Take your time, hun, and let me know if you want anything."

I step inside the dressing room with an armful of garments, running my fingertips across the fabrics as I walk. I close the door behind me and take a deep breath, gazing around at the racks of clothing. The colors are vibrant and the cuts are flattering; I want so desperately to buy everything. I arrange the outfits on hangers and begin trying them one by one, turning in front of the mirror as I admire how they fit. It's been so long since I've gone on a shopping spree.

As I prepare to zip of a short tight one-piece dress, I realize the zipper is low on my back. I try to reach behind me to zip it up, but my fingers fall short. I peek out the door and with a pang of disappointment realize that the that the dressing room attendant is nowhere in sight.

Dante's nearby, and he's checking his cell. He looks up when he sees me. "What do you need?"

"Just some help with a zipper. Is the attendant nearby?" I ask.

He peeks around the corner and then comes back. "Nope. Helping another lady. I can give you a hand." He slipped his cell phone in his pocket.

"Um...okay but..." I look around. "Be quick. I think the dressing room is for ladies only."

He slips inside and I promptly close the door. He surveyed me in the intricately detailed dress, his eyes twinkling with admiration. "Valeria, that gown looks amazing on you," he said, as he adjusted the straps of my gown and carefully tucked in the fabric around my neck.

"Thank you." I blush. "I think I'll get it then."

I catch a glimpse of our reflections in the mirror, and in that moment, I see us not as two people from different worlds, but as two individuals entwined by a complex fate.

"Now just help me unzip."

He slowly drags the zipper down my back, his fingers teasingly caressing my spine. My heart races as he draws ever closer. I feel his warm breath on my neck and I melt back into his chest.

The space right near us came alive with laughter and chatter from a group of ladies. Acting quickly, I pull him back behind the wall portion and press his body tightly against it to make sure his feet are hidden. "Shh," I say, my voice barely audible.

"What—" I press a finger to his lips before he can say anything else to give away that he's in the dressing room with me.

The ladies move away from our stall, but Dante holds my finger to his lips and sucks it into his mouth.

"Dante," I warn, my body heating up.

"Take off the dress already, Valeria," he says.

"What?"

I could feel my heart pounding in my chest as I stand frozen, unable to break free from his captivating gaze. Before I know what is happening he had already pulled the straps of my dress away from my shoulders. The fabric of my dress disappears in a single tug, leaving me exposed and vulnerable. He picks me up by the waist and then stands me on the seating bend. With his powerful hands he pins me against the wall of the stall, crushing my body against its cold surface.

"Oh my God, Dante, they'll hear us," I whisper.

He tightens his grip on my waist and leans in close, his breath hot against my ear. "Then you better be quiet," he whispers.

He raises his hand behind me and I tense, bracing for the sound of an open palm against my skin, but instead his fingers massage my ass. He releases me and pull back slightly to meet my gaze. "Besides if we're going to be together, we're not going to hide it."

I bite down hard on my lips to suppress the moans that threaten to escape. He firmly grips my ass cheeks and devours me hungrily from behind. His tongue laps at my clit, slides into my slit, and teases my ass before winding around my anus in tantalizing circles. I'm careful not to make a sound, but then he slides two fingers inside my juicy pussy.

"Fucking wet ass cunt," he whispers against my ass, running his tongue inside. "I should fuck your tight pussy in this dressing room."

I reach back and grab his hands which are on my ass. "Dante, please..."

He proceeds to tongue me until my legs are shaking and my juices are running down my legs and onto the bench. I know he's trying to make me cry out and he gets his wish. I cum so hard I'm not able to hold in the violent cry that rips from my throat. My orgasm comes by surprise. I quickly stifle my squeals of pleasure as best I can.

When he's through with me, he licks his lips, straightens his blazer, and adjusts his hard crotch.

"I'm not done with you yet," he says just before he exits the dressing stall.

Trembling, I get dressed and bring out the garments. He's standing right outside the door. He grins when I walk past on legs that feel like jello and follows me silently till we reach the cashier. The stares we get from the attendant and the other ladies say it all. They know exactly what happened in that dressing room. I don't think I'll ever forget.

Just as I think we are done after the driver and his attendant places our shopping bags in the trunk, Dante takes my hand and helps me inside the car. The smell of his cologne fills my nose and his familiar warmth wraps around me like a comforting blanket.

Before I can utter a word, he grabs my throat in that special way he always does and captures my mouth with his own. His kiss is filled with passion that leaves my head spinning. His fingers slide between my thighs, seeking out my innermost secrets. He mumbles against my lips, "I told you I wasn't done yet."

My heart races as anticipation builds inside me. He unbuckles his belt and shoves his pants down, revealing his nine-inch dick free from its confinement. It's already full of life.

The windows of the car are deeply tinted and emptiness surrounds us on the back lot where it's been parked. Dante flips me over and props me on my hands and knees on the back seat of the car. He grabs my hair into a tight ponytail with his fist and plunges himself balls deep inside. I immediately scream out in pleasure. My pussy is still raw and swollen from him sucking on it. He fucks me hard and fast and when he's done the driver and his attendant slip right back inside as if they knew not to enter and then knew when to do so.

All the way back to the lake house, Dante's hand is on my thigh possessively and the other hand is on his cell phone messaging away. He can deliver pleasure and fun and get business done all at the same time. I found that shit so sexy. I'm floating on Cloud nine.

Twenty-Three

Valeria

I wake up to the sound of the engine roaring to life, my senses immediately alert. I glance at the clock, realizing it's still early in the morning. As I groggily get out of bed—Dante's bed—my eyes widen at the sight of him and his men getting into a sleek black Maserati parked outside in the front.

Somehow he had slipped out of my arms before the break of dawn and snuck off. I frowned. A pang of disappointment and frustration tugs at my heart.

I know exactly what this means—Dante is leaving again, leaving me behind without a word. I can't deny the sting of his absence, the feeling of being left in the dark. But I also understand the nature of his business, the demands it places on his time and attention.

Turning away from the window, my gaze lands on a vivid red package resting on the dresser. I take a step closer and inspect it. It's wrapped up tight in fancy paper that glistens in the morning light. My heart beating fast, I hesitantly unwrap it.

Inside, I find a brand new laptop customized just for me. I wrapped the smaller box and instantly smile when I see the necklace that I tried on at the outlet—the one I thought was too expensive for me. For a moment, I forget that I'm supposed to be disturbed about him leaving here.

I pick up the note with the gifts and read Dante's message. *'Taking care of business. Be back soon.'*

I can't deny the practicality of the laptop, a gesture ensuring I can continue my work while he's away. And the necklace, a symbol of his affection and thoughtfulness, serves as a constant reminder of his presence, even when physically absent.

I take a deep breath, letting the weight of the situation settle within me. I knew what I was getting into when I allowed myself to open up to Dante and when I asked him to open up to me.

Beside revenge for something I did in self defense, I still don't know what he wants from me.

Twenty-Four

Dante

The sleek black car glides through the bustling city streets, the sounds of traffic merging with the low hum of the engine. Vito sits beside me, his eyes focused on the road ahead. We're on our way to meet with one of my clients, the urgency of the situation pressing upon me like a heavy weight on my shoulders.

Silence envelops us for a moment, broken only by the rhythm of the car's movement. And then, unexpectedly, Vito's voice cuts through the air, piercing the quiet. "Dante, what are your intentions with Valeria?" His words hang in the air, the weight of his question making me uneasy.

I'm aware he has caught sight of us being in each other's company. I'm equally aware that he knows that I have taken care of the amenities to make her time at the mansion with me more comfortable.

I turn to face Vito, his unwavering gaze meeting mine. His loyalty and honesty are qualities I cherish, more than mere words can express. I take a moment to consider his question, aware that my answer could have far-reaching consequences.

"I plan to make Valeria my wife."

The words hang in the air, echoing between us. Vito's brows furrow slightly, a mix of concern and caution etched on his face.

"You are playing a very dangerous game, Dante," Vito warns, his voice tinged with worry. His words hold the weight of wisdom, a cautionary reminder of the perils that await.

I meet his gaze with a steady stare, a glimmer of defiance in my eyes.

"Love and war, Vito," I reply, my voice laced with determination. "What else do I have to live for?" The words escape my lips with a sense of both resignation and longing.

Vito nods, his expression a blend of understanding and concern. It's a silent acknowledgement of the risks I'm willing to take, the sacrifices I'm prepared to make. He knows me better than anyone, aware of the void that exists within me, a void that only Valeria seems capable of filling. Even if she doesn't understand me, she seeks to understand.

As the car continues its journey through the city, my mind is consumed by a tumultuous mix of emotions. Lust, loyalty, duty, and the relentless pursuit of power intertwine within me, creating a tapestry of inner conflict. Yet, despite the dangers that lie ahead, I can't deny the pull of my heart, the desire to claim Valeria as my own.

Twenty-Five

Dante

The warehouse is dimly lit, and the smell of gunpowder enhances the tense atmosphere. I take in the sight of the lifeless bodies strewn about the concrete floor, a reminder of what had just transpired. My heart thumps faster as I look around, my adrenaline spiking. I survey the aftermath of the shootout.

Vito joins me at the edge of the room. His eyes meet mine, reflecting a mix of exhaustion and determination. We both know that this operation was more than a simple gang dispute. The evidence we've uncovered connects the Nighthawks to the disappearance of Rick Johnson who was trying to untangle himself from an embezzlement scheme.

As we approach one of the fallen assailants, my gaze lands on a wallet sticking out one's back pocket. I snatch it out and set it beside me, trying to ignore its wetness. Opening the wallet, my eyes widen at the sight of familiar identification belonging to Rick Johnson. He's dead. I kick the body and it rolls over. Sure enough, Johnson's lifeless eyes are colorless. But something looks off. This man hasn't just died as a result of the shootout. He's been dead for hours, maybe days. Looks like from the deep gash in his throat. There's lots of bloating around his abdomen. It confirms our suspicions—the missing partner's involvement in this dangerous web.

Vito joins me and looks down at Johnson. "The dead don't speak, Dante."

Suddenly, a cell phone buried among someone's body rings, shattering the heavy silence. Instinctively, I reach for it, a hunch guiding my actions. Without hesitation, I answer the call in Italian, my voice steady but brimming with tension.

"Well, is it done? Did you find Leonardo Argentieri's triple stash?" a voice on the other end demands.

My muscles tense at the mention of my father's name, but I can't reveal the turmoil raging within me. Suppressing the surge of emotions, I reply in a controlled tone, "Negative. Need more time."

The unknown caller curses in frustration, their words laced with urgency. "You've got twenty-four fucking hours to bring me something. Word is they have the Cipriano princess in their clutches. Get to her. She's my blood. See what she's learned. You know what to do."

Anger simmers within me, threatening to consume my every thought. I end the call abruptly, knowing the caller has no idea he's been talking to the wrong man all this time. He's been talking to Leonardo Argentieri's son himself.

Valeria, my Valeria, entangled in this twisted game? The revelation sends shockwaves through my soul, a mix of disbelief and betrayal gripping my heart.

Vito, always perceptive, approaches from behind, his voice laced with heavy suspicion. "I heard all that. Something tells me the Ciprianos are responsible in the end for this mess," he remarks, holding up a pocket knife bearing the Cipriano family crest that he discovered. The implication hangs heavily in the air, shattering the illusion of Valeria's innocence.

I clench my fists, my knuckles turning white as conflicting emotions swirl within me. Valeria, the woman who captivated my heart, now connected to a web of deceit and danger. Whether knowingly or unknowingly, I don't know. The questions multiply, and I find myself torn between loyalty and the truth I seek.

In the face of mounting uncertainty, one thing remains clear—the pieces of this intricate puzzle are falling into place, revealing a treacherous connection between Valeria, the Cipriano family, and my own bloodline.

The cards have been dealt...probably not in my favor.

Twenty-Six

Dante

I sit alone in my dimly lit basement office, surrounded by stacks of papers and evidence. The weight of the world rests upon my shoulders as I delve deeper into the tangled web of deceit. The revelations I've uncovered have sent shockwaves through my soul, shaking the very foundation of my trust.

Every piece of evidence I've unearthed points to the involvement of the Cipriano family, and the embezzlement, disappearance, and killing of Johnson. Some top dog somewhere is responsible for all this. It's a damning realization, and the implications threaten to shatter the fragile trust I have in Valeria, trying to find out why the caller on the other end wanted his contact to reach her. Has she or will she knowingly provided information or intel that would be my downfall? Or is she innocent of this mess?

As the minutes tick by, the sound of footsteps breaks the silence, drawing me back to the present.

Valeria enters the basement office, her voice cutting through the air. "How long have you been back?" she asks, her tone laced with a mixture of surprise and disappointment.

I keep my attention fixed on the papers in front of me, avoiding her penetrating gaze. "Since last night," I reply curtly, my voice devoid of emotion.

"And you didn't say anything." Her voice tinged with hurt and frustration. Her words hang in the air, a tangible reminder of the distance that has grown between us.

The weight of her disappointment settles upon my shoulders, a heavy burden I cannot ignore.

"You shouldn't be down here," I say, my voice firm but laced with a hint of vulnerability.

She folds her arms across her chest. "Has a switch flipped? What's wrong? You don't want to fuck me anymore? I'm just a throwaway girl."

I bite my lip. I know she is tenacious, unwilling to back down from a confrontation. It's one of the things that drew me to her, but now it only adds to the tension between us.

Unyielding, she barges into the room, her eyes blazing with defiance. I rise from my desk, meeting her fiery gaze head-on. After all, there's not telling if she might shoot me or stab me. She's done these things before.

"Dante," she begins, her voice filled with frustration, "What's going on? Did I do something?"

The questions hang in the air, each word striking a chord deep within me. The rift between us widens, and the truth I've discovered weighs heavily on my heart. I take a step closer, my voice tinged with a mix of anguish and determination.

"Valeria," I say, my voice trembling with suppressed emotions, "Your family's past, maybe your family altogether makes me weary of trusting you. I don't know what your intentions—"

"What the hell do you mean? You don't know my intentions?" she shoots back.

"When you were sent here four years ago, what was your mission?" I ask point blank.

She shakes her head. "What mission? I was fourteen! I didn't know what the fuck was going on. My father sold me like a common slave and your father locked me away in a room so he could fuck me...hmmm...sounds like someone else I know. And—"

"Don't!" I hold up a hand. "Don't ever compare me to my father!"

A mixture of hurt and confusion flickers across Valeria's face. "I never asked for any of this," she whispers, her voice barely above a breath. "After I was sold to your horny-ass daddy, my entire family was murdered in Italy in cold blood. I couldn't even get to them, to their funerals to mourn them because your fucking lieutenants were after me. I was scared for my fucking life. I was fourteen. I had no fucking one."

The pain in her eyes mirrors my own, and for a moment, the walls that have risen between us crumble. "Valeria..."

She picks up a vase of roses and throws it across the room and it shatters on the floor. "I wanted to be left alone, so don't fucking stand there and act like I just pussy-footed my way into your life to ruin yours. You took me. You kidnapped me!"

"I know." I sigh, cautiously coming toward her.

"Stay back!" Tears are streaming down her face; her makeup is in streaks on her rosy cheeks.

"Valeria, I—"

"I can't understand you, Dante, so whatever it is you think I'm trying to do behind your back, I hope you put on your little private investigator hat and figure it out your damn self," she scowls.

"I've been doing that—" She doesn't let me finish.

"*Go fuck yourself!*"

She twists around on her heels and storms out of the office. Doors slam as she makes her way back on the stairs.

Fuck. I feel stupid as fuck. Valeria is likely innocent, but if she is, that means she has no idea what her family is up to. That makes it much harder for me to gain the upper hand. That makes it much harder for me to protect her, knowing fully well that they're now after her too.

Twenty-Seven

Valeria

I spend the next couple of days in a state of turmoil, avoiding Dante's presence whenever possible. Guilt gnaws at my conscience, as I begin to wonder if my family has crossed paths with him in ways I can't fathom. Had he known all of this before kidnapping me?

My past, the life of a Cipriano princess, feels like a distant memory. I had believed everyone thought I was dead, and I no longer identified myself with that surname. Yet, Dante seems convinced that I am involved in the turmoil that has unfolded, that I was sent four years ago to spy on him, his father, and their dealings. It couldn't be further from the truth.

The loneliness begins to weigh on me. I have caught a glimpse of what a real relationship can be, and I can't bear the thought of losing it. The sweeter side of Dante, the moments of tenderness we shared, still linger in my mind. I want to find a way to make things right, to bridge the gap that has grown between us, even though I have no clear solution.

Just as I start to lose hope, the silence in my room is shattered by the sound of the door bursting open. My heart leaps to my throat, anticipating another round of interrogation. But to my surprise, it is Dante standing in the doorway, his eyes fierce and dark.

"We're going to a dinner fundraiser gala," he declares, his voice leaving no room for argument. "Get dressed. Be ready downstairs in one hour."

His words catch me off guard, the sudden change in his demeanor leaving me momentarily stunned. I expected anger and accusation, not an invitation to a social event. Confusion clouds my thoughts as I struggle to comprehend his intentions.

Before I can gather my wits and respond, he turns on his heel and leaves the room, leaving me standing there, a mix of apprehension and curiosity swirling within me. What does this mean? Is he trying to bridge the gap between us or merely using this event as a ruse to further his investigations?

Either way, it's better than staying on the property all day. I'm constantly surrounded by more than one guard at all times because Dante suddenly thinks that someone will take me away from him. Imagine that. The kidnapper thinks his kidnappee will be kidnapped by someone else. I can't make this stuff up.

With a deep breath, I push aside my inner conflict and begin to prepare for the evening that holds the promise of both reconciliation and revelations.

Twenty-Eight

Valeria

The grandeur of the gala unfolds before us as we step into the opulent ballroom. It's a spectacle of wealth and influence, with the rich, famous, and elite from every major US city gathered in one place. The setting is a magnificent blend of sophistication and extravagance. Crystal chandeliers cast a soft, shimmering light across the room, illuminating the finely dressed guests as they mingle and socialize. The air is alive with the sound of laughter, clinking glasses, and the enchanting melodies of a live orchestra.

I attended these with my mother the year before she died. Only because my father was never around to go with her. Business and all that stuff. She loved the events. It gave her a chance to mingle with other socialites in Italy. Yet, I understand the appeal of it. If I was in a business capacity, like Dante is, or even as an entrepreneur, I would be engaging with many investors. There are many here.

Dante remains quiet, his eyes ever-roaming across the crowd, observing and assessing with a keen sense of awareness. It dawns on me that this outing may be about more than just a simple night out. There is an undercurrent of purpose in his demeanor, a hidden agenda that piques my curiosity and fuels my own inner conflict.

Before we left, I decided to put my irritation with him aside. I was so angry at his lack of faith in me and felt the need to express it somewhere. Hence, why I felt the need to vent in his basement office.

For a while, I manage to set aside my unease and immerse myself in the atmosphere. I enjoy the fleeting moments of bliss that come from being surrounded by such elegance and glamour.

But then, amidst the sea of unfamiliar faces, I catch a glimpse of someone I think I know. A male cousin. Or maybe my eyes are playing tricks on me. It's strange seeing him here since the last time I saw him was in Italy at my father's place before I was sold away.

Our eyes meet, and I see flickers of familiarity and curiosity in his gaze as he discreetly glances in my direction. Panic surges through me, and my heart skips a beat. Is it my family? Is my cousin really here. They call him Enzo, but I know he has a twin brother. Twins run in our family.

I clasp my fingers around Dante's forearm to get his attention as we fall in line to be seated for meals. "Dante?"

He leans down and whispers, "What is it, Valeria?"

"I see someone I know. He's from Italy. He's family."

"Where?"

"To the right. By the bar. He's in a dark gray suit with the blue tie," I say.

Dante glances over discreetly. "No one like that is near the bar."

I glance up to and he's right. Enzo is gone.

"Wait." Dante squeezes my arm gently. "Does he have short beard? Is he lanky? Does he have a grin wider than a crook's?"

"I...yes."

"I see him." Dante presses his palm gently into my back. "Stay close to me. Okay?"

I nod. "I will."

Once they seat us, Dante pulls his chair closer to mine and places his hand possessively over my thigh, just like he always does. This time I slip my hand in his as it rests on my lap.

As the speaker talks, my attention wanes and my mind spins with thoughts and questions that seem to have no answers. The events of the past weeks unravel a web of secrets, alliances, and conflicts that I never could have anticipated. The Cipriano family, my own family, their sudden interest in me feels like a betrayal, a twisted game of power and control. All this time they could've been searching for me when I needed it most. They could've saved me from myself. I wonder why my family desires me, what hidden motives lie behind their actions. Are they merely seeking to exploit my connection with Dante, to gain leverage over him? Or is there something more sinister at play?

I gaze across the dining hall, but I see no signs of Enzo, but I do see Dante's security. I know he's texted them once or twice as I'd seen him pull out his phone while we were being seating.

In my heart, I know that Dante and I are caught in the middle of a dangerous game, a power struggle that threatens to consume us both. The world of mafia made men is ruthless and unforgiving, where loyalty and alliances are constantly shifting like sand. I have seen the consequences firsthand, the bloodshed and heartbreak that accompany such feuds. I know that a war is brewing, and I fear that I am already entangled in its destructive path.

But despite the looming darkness, a fierce determination burns within me. I will not willingly betray Dante, no matter the circumstances or the pressures that surround us. He has shown me a glimpse of something I might never see before with anyone else.

As I trace the edge of the ruby necklace that rests against my skin, I feel a surge of defiance. The Cipriano family may have their own plans and schemes, but I refuse to be a pawn anymore in anyone's game. I will fight for my own agency, my own freedom, and the complex bond that has blossomed between Dante and me.

Seizing a moment when most of the table is engrossed in a speaker's speech, I lean over towards Dante, whispering under my breath, "Did you know, Dante?"

"That there was a Cipriano on the guest list?" he whispers back. "No. I have a piece being auctioned off for the fundraiser afterward, but we won't be there to see it."

The speaker announces the end of the event and walks off the podium.

"We're leaving," Dante states.

We navigate through the lingering crowd, I can feel Dante's urgency radiating from him like a palpable force.

His grip on my hand tightens, his eyes scanning the room with a steely determination. I can sense his unwavering focus, his only aim now to get us out of here, away from lurking dangers.

"If I were here without you, things would be different," Dante murmurs under his breath, his voice laced with frustration and restrained anger. "I would've confronted that bastard who's been eyeing you all night about what I know and raised hell."

His words send a shiver down my spine, both from the intensity of his emotions and the implications they carry. My family, as they were in the past, has always been a formidable force, their reputation preceding them. I know firsthand the consequences of crossing them, the price one pays for defiance. Yet, Dante's unwavering spirit, his refusal to bow down, both terrifies and exhilarates me.

As we push through the throng of guests, Dante presses his cell phone against his ear, his voice commanding and urgent as he speaks to his driver, instructing them to pull up the car. After he pushes the phone back down into his blazer's inside pocket, he uses his other free hand to grasp his gun. He doesn't pull it out in public.

I cling to him, my heart pounding in my chest, fear rising within me like a tempest. I can't help but look around, my eyes darting from one face to another, searching for any sign of danger, any glimpse of Enzo who was once an enforcer in my father's ranks. He probably even knows more about my father's murder than I do.

The grand hall seems to close in on me, the air thick with tension. As we near the exit, my gaze locks onto Enzo standing next to a white limousine. A sense of foreboding tightens its grip on my heart, warning me that things are about to go awry. Panic begins to rise within me, threatening to extinguish all hope.

A second passes after Dante sees Enzo and chaos erupts. The air is suddenly filled with the sounds of screeching tires and gunfire. It's an ambush. People are screaming and flying out of the way. Guests are running back into the building to take cover. After a while, the only people left in the courtyard are Enzo and his men and Dante and his men.

"Stay with me," Dante urges.

Dante rushes forward, shoving me into the shadows of his sleek Maserati. Vito extends a hand to drag me away from harm and into the waiting car, but my mind is incapacitated with fear and dread. I slip out of his grasp, desperately scanning for a glimpse of Dante amidst the horror. It is in that single moment of indecision that Dante throws himself in front of me, an act of protection to save me from the spray of bullets. Dante's body jolts, his face distorted with agonizing pain.

"Oh no," I wail.

"Go, get in the car," Dante bites out, shoving me towards it.

The back and forth shots continue between both sides. Dante and Vito fire back, lying down three men in front of the white limo. My heart plummets, my breath catching in my throat as I witness the impact of this terror. Fear and anguish intertwine within me, threatening to consume everything.

Suddenly, five men jump into the white limo and it takes off. The gunshots stop. I rush to Dante's side, my hands trembling as I cradle his wounded form.

"Is he hurt bad?" I gasp. *Oh, please don't let him be hurt badly.* My mind races as I picture all of the horrible possibilities, until it feels like my anguish will consume me.

"He's fine. Get him in the car. You get in the car too. Right now." Vito points to the open door. By the tone of his voice, I can tell that I'm in no position to not listen.

Vito and his men manage to get him in the Maserati, laying him next tome with his head on my lap. The Maserati speeds off as two men work with a medical kit to stop Dante's bleeding. Police sirens are wailing in the distance. The world blurs around us as we navigate through the night.

Dante's eyes flutter open, and his arm trembles as he lifts it slowly to my face. His fingertips brushed against my skin like a whisper, and I smile with relief to see his eager gaze.

My fingertips linger on his face. "Dante."

"I'm here," he said, his voice deep and comforting.

I breathed heavily, my face close to his own. "I was scared."

He smiled gently. "Don't worry. I won't let you fall."

Twenty-Nine

Valeria

Dante's injuries force him to remain confined to his bed for several agonizing days. He is still fighting to get up and pick up where he left off but the doctors don't recommend it.

I find myself torn between a mix of emotions—worry for Dante's well-being, frustration at the situation we find ourselves in, and an overwhelming sense of determination to support him through this ordeal. It felt like an unending battle between my conflicting emotions.

The muted light of the bedside lamp illuminated Dante's troubled face as he slept, a thin sheen of sweat covering his brow. Thank God the gunshot wasn't serious or fatal. His private doctors have been coming and going throughout the day and their only concerns were blood and fluid lost. All he needed was a bit of time to recover.

I sit in the chair by his side, taking care to keep my movements quiet and not disturb him. Soft music drifted from the speakers on the wall, a gentle reminder that beyond these four walls, life was still going on. Vito, his underboss, and other lieutenants have already made arrangements to keep the business operating as he rests.

Dante's eyes suddenly open, and he attempts to sit up, reaching to his right. I suppose he's reaching for his gun. Vito took it earlier. They don't allow the gun in the room while I'm in here with Vito and I know why. I don't blame them. They still don't trust me.

I quickly press my hands onto Dante's chest and firmly but gently hold him in place.

"Dante, you should stay lying down," I whisper. "Doctor's orders."

He smirks in response. "I don't take orders from anyone. Feels like I've slept five hundred days or something like that," he chuckles.

I can't help but laugh too. "Not really."

I hand Dante a glass of water and he takes it before swinging his legs over the bed but not standing up.

"Dante..." I warn, knowing what he is about to do.

"I'm okay, Valeria," He insists confidently as he wraps his strong arms around me and leans in for a kiss. Then he parts and takes a few seconds to look at me, folding a stray hair behind my ear and away from my face. The warmth of his touch brings an instant comfort to me—one that had been missing for days. "And I'm glad you're okay too."

"I'm so sorry. I was trying to get to you. I should have listened." I can't even look at him when I say this, but he tips my chin and makes me.

"It's not your fault. What was going to happen was going to happen. If anything, it's my fault. I shouldn't have taken you there."

"But I want to be with you," I say.

"Valeria, your family is after you and I don't know if that's a good thing or bad thing."

I shake my head. "My family sold me away when I was a child, so what do you think?"

Dante sighs. Just as I think he's about to speak, the door swings open, and Vito, steps into the room.

They exchange a glance, a silent understanding passing between them, before engaging in a conversation that sounds like a coded language, filled with cryptic references and veiled meanings. It's a language born out of necessity, a shield against prying ears and hidden dangers.

Dante's jaw clenches as he declares, "We've gotta meet 'em head on."

Vito quickly shakes his head in disagreement, worry lines crossing his forehead. "We could be walking into a trap."

"You've got a point, but the ball's in my court, Vito. Look what they did. They started shit they can't finish." Dante turns away, determination hardening his expression.

I strain to catch other uncoded snippets of their conversation, trying to piece together the puzzle they're unraveling. They discuss various dealings, the decisions Vito has made in Dante's absence, their voices hushed and guarded.

Vito's eyes widen as he mutters, "Makes me wonder who's behind the Johnson embezzlement scheme."

"Johnson could've been a puppet or a distraction," Dante replies, a hint of sarcasm seeping through his words. He makes a dismissive gesture with one hand. "Can't ask him now any way but I have a suspicion on where this leads."

Vito arches an eyebrow quizzically. "Ciprianos?"

My heart skips a beat, my breath catching in my throat. What can they be discussing? What secrets lay hidden in the shadows that I know nothing about? I silently watch as their exchange continue to unfold. They continue speaking in code, their words a dance of evasion and discretion.

Vito turns his eyes towards me, a hint of suspicion on his face. Sensing the unspoken request in his eyes, I find myself caught between the desire to know the truth and the instinct to respect Dante's boundaries.

"Valeria, if you don't mind," Vito starts. "I need to have a word with Dante. *Alone.*"

Dante remains silent, his eyes meeting mine with a conflicted intensity. I can see the battle raging within him, the struggle to reconcile the trust he once placed in me with the ever-present shadow of doubt that has clouded our relationship since my arrival.

"It's okay," I finally say, my voice barely above a whisper. "I can come back later."

The memories of our tumultuous history surface, intertwined with the grief that still lingers from the loss of my father. The uncertainty of what might have been, had fate dealt us a different hand, hangs heavy in the room.

But deep down, I know that despite the circumstances that brought me here, the bond that has grown between us is real. But would it be broken?

With a heavy heart, I step away from the bedside, allowing Vito and Dante the privacy they seek. As I make my way towards the door, I can't help but wonder what secrets lie behind their veiled words, what dangers loom on the horizon.

Thirty

Dante

As Valeria leaves the room, a heaviness settles upon me, a weight that encompasses both the physical pain and the burden of the choices I must make. Vito and I are left alone, the air charged with tension and the gravity of our conversation.

Vito meets my gaze, his eyes reflecting the same determination that burns within me. We both know that this is a critical moment, a juncture where we must navigate the treacherous waters of betrayal and deceit. We need to unravel the truth, to understand this complicated web and the motives.

"Vito," I begin, my voice laced with both weariness and urgency, "we have to dig deeper. Maybe start with the embezzlement. Find out who else might be involved, who stands to benefit from this scheme."

Vito nods, his expression serious. "I've already started pulling some strings, Dante. There are rumors circulating Johnson, particular with his banker. Guys hands are tied because his shit is heavily regulated by the feds now. He could've been a pawn just like you said."

"But for which top dog?" I ask, inquisitively.

"We're gonna find out." Vito strokes his chin. "The Ciprianos...they have a sudden interest in Valeria now. They probably knew she was alive, so why go after her now after you've just found her?"

I shake my head. "Valeria admits to no wrongdoing. She doesn't know. She's been out of the loop for four years or so she says so how can she know?"

The Ciprianos and their sudden interest in Valeria have raised more questions than answers. Why do they want her back? What secrets lie hidden within her past? The possibilities, each more dangerous than the last, race through my mind.

"They want Valeria for something," I muse aloud, frustration seeping into my voice. "But what?"

"Leverage?" Vito offers.

"Fuck." I run my fingers through my hair. "I mean, shit, they don't know what's going on between us."

Vito is quiet for a while and then says, "It's not like you've been hiding anything, D. You've been fucking her in every corner of the house and taking her out in the city."

I exhaled loudly.

Vito slumps down on the sofa. "You know your father intended Valeria for himself."

I point at him. "No. You don't know that."

Vito raised one shoulder in a shrug. "I mean, come on. Valeria was young and fertile. Leonardo got her here and was about to fuck her. Isn't that what you said?"

"She was too young. It wouldn't have happened right away," I say.

"Of course not, but your father was in very very good health. All he had was time to wait. Marco's not a dumb man. He knew that if Valeria produced a heir, it would still have Cipriano blood. Ciprianos and Argentieris would be connected by blood."

My anger rose at his words, and I jumped up from the bed, my back to him as I stared out the window towards the setting sun.

"D, you have to consider every possibility. If Valeria had been brought here for the sole purpose of producing heirs for Leonardo, it would have happened eventually—if she hadn't shot him point-blank first. But she did. And then her father was whacked. That means there wouldn't have been any solid evidence of an agreement of intended exchange of assets between the Argentieri and Cipriano families, which would put an end to the peace agreement. The impasse they agreed on, remember?"

My fists clenched tightly at my sides. "I wasn't there making the agreement, so I don't know what it entailed. Just as you predict, it wasn't even in writing as far as I know. You're right, deal is squashed."

Vito studied me silently before offering another thought. "You know what...? Not necessarily. Not if Valeria's father had chosen someone to take his place before he was murdered..."

I turned around and met his gaze directly, realizing just how serious the implication I was about to make truly was. "Or if there were already plans in motion for someone else to take over."

Vito leans against the edge of a nearby table, his gaze fixed on me with unwavering loyalty. "We'll get to the bottom of it, D."

The weight of responsibility settles upon my shoulders, the weight of leadership and the choices that define us. I've faced countless battles in this world of power and shadows, but this feels different, more personal.

Valeria's presence in my life has awakened emotions I thought were long buried, vulnerabilities that both frighten and exhilarate me.

Amidst the discussion, an undercurrent of unease tugs at my thoughts. I know the struggles within my own heart, the battle between trust and doubt that Valeria's presence has ignited.

I don't know how this will end. But until it ends...I'm fighting for what's mine.

Valeria Cipriano is mine. No one's going to take her from me.

Thirty-One

Valeria

I carefully carry a tray with a steaming plate of dinner towards Dante's office. The aroma fills the air, mixing with the soft glow of the desk lamp.

Dante's presence dominates the space, his eyes focused on papers and documents scattered across his desk. It's become a familiar sight—Dante spending countless hours here, immersed in his work, his attention consumed by the affairs of his empire.

His aloofness stings, the avoidance of any discussions regarding my family becoming more apparent. I can't help but wonder what he's hiding, whether he's investigating them in secret or having clandestine conversations with Vito about it.

Dante's piercing gaze meets mine as I approach and he grins. "What do we have here?"

I place the tray on the desk and he shoves some papers aside to receive it.

"I thought you might be hungry."

"For plenty of things, yes," he says, rubbing his hands together. "But we can start with this first."

I grin and blush, knowing exactly what he means. If there's one thing that Dante doesn't pass up on, it's sex. Most nights are quick and intense, but other nights he takes his time with me. He doesn't let me bring up our troubles during, before or after our sessions—ever. I'm okay with that, but I know sooner or later we'll have to face the bad stuff.

He tilted his head up and pressed his lips to mine, sending a warm shiver down my spine. He then pulled me onto his lap so that I was facing away from him, and gently trailed butterfly kisses across the back of my neck.

"You know, if I weren't expecting Vito any minute, I'd fuck you while you're on my lap and eat dinner at the same time," he teases.

I giggled. "Of course you would, Mr. multi-tasker."

"That's me."

I allow him to eat for a while and I even share a few nibbles of his food that he offers on a fork. I love the way he eats. I can tell he's never had table manners from some fancy school like the one I went to, but that's okay. He's quite cute to me.

"What's on your mind?" he asks, suddenly, shifting me on his lap so that I was inward.

"How did you know something was on my mind?" I shouldn't be surprised. My face is like an open book. I wouldn't be a very good poke player.

"Dante," I begin, my voice gentle yet tinged with a hint of frustration, "I wanted to tell you something. Something that's been bothering me."

Dante puts the fork down, leans back, and looks up, his gaze meeting mine briefly.

"Right before you took me, I had a ticket to Italy," I continue, my voice trembling.

"I know."

"What?" I'm taken back.

"I know you were planning a flight. That's why I made my move that day. That's why your boss told you it was urgent...because I told him it was urgent."

My mouth parts and I frown, gathering my thoughts. "You're not lying about being a good investigator, are you?"

He tilts his head to the side. "Valeria, something you should understand that even before I took my father's place as boss, I had work in the business. My father was good at delegating more than investigating and uncovering shit, so I did that work for him."

I nod. "No wonder."

"So, what were you going to Italy for?"

"Well, that's the thing. I wanted to uncover the truth about why my father, my stepmom, and my little brothers were killed and by whom. Something kept bothering me over the years. I wasn't supposed to leave until the next morning, not the night my father was killed. Dante, I think someone in my family knew that my father was going to be executed. My maid rushed me out of the house. She put me on that helicopter and then I never saw my father again."

"Hmmm." Dante stroked his chin. "That does change things. Your father's murder must've been planned."

I nod. "Yes. I might have been among the dead if they hadn't gotten me out."

"Maybe. Maybe not."

The weight of those words hangs heavy in the room, the silence thick with unspoken fears and unanswered questions. We both realize the danger that looms over us, the sinister intentions of the Cipriano family threatening to engulf our lives in chaos.

"Why haven't you confided in me about anything that you know?" I ask, my voice betraying a mix of concern and hurt. "We're in this together, Dante. Whatever concerns my family, concerns me. I'm already involved, whether you like it or not."

Dante's eyes finally meet mine, his expression hardened. "Valeria, this is grown men's business," he says, his voice firm. "I can't get women tangled up in this. Especially not you. I brought you here. It's my duty to protect you while you remain here."

His words sting, a painful reminder of the boundaries he draws between us. I understand his intentions, his desire to shield me from the dark underbelly of his life, but I can't help but feel a twinge of resentment. I'm not a fragile flower to be sheltered. My own family's involvement in this world has left its mark on me, and I refuse to be left in the dark.

His rough hand finds its way to my hair and sweeps it back as he speaks, "Just know this, Valeria," he said, "if anyone is jeopardizing my business and legacy, I won't stand idly by.

I won't let them destroy what my family has built. I'll have no choice but to take them down."

He pulls back slightly and lowers his hand to my cheek, thumb grazing over my skin, before pressing his lips to my forehead in a tender gesture that belies the force of his words.

"I understand and respect that."

"But I can't let you go, Valeria," he says, his voice filled with a mix of desperation and resolve. "If it comes to it, I'll start a war to make you my wife. I won't lose you."

Thirty-Two

Dante

The bustling casino floor stretches out before us, a kaleidoscope of flashing lights and the constant hum of voices. It's a world of decadence and desire, where fortunes are made and lost with the turn of a card or the spin of a wheel. But tonight, amidst the glittering facade, a storm is brewing.

I lead my men through the crowd, our presence commanding attention. We're a force to be reckoned with, the air crackling with the raw energy of imminent danger. The patrons and staff cast curious glances our way, their whispers floating through the air like fleeting echoes.

"Keep your eyes sharp," I say to my men, my voice low but commanding. "We need to find the private room without drawing unnecessary attention."

We navigate through the maze of slot machines and gaming tables, our steps purposeful and swift. The scent of cigars and expensive perfumes mingle in the air, adding to the atmosphere of opulence and excess. The tension is high, as if the walls themselves hold their breath, anticipating the clash that is about to unfold.

I know why I'm here. I've found a rat bastard. I've found Enzo Cipriano.

As we approach the entrance to the private room, two security guards stand sentry, their imposing figures blocking our way. I exchange a knowing glance with Vito, and he steps forward, his voice smooth but commanding.

"Gentlemen, I believe we have an arrangement," Vito says, his tone laced with confidence.

The guards exchange a brief look before nodding and stepping aside. The path is clear, and we move forward with a sense of purpose. The heavy door to the private room stands before us, its polished wood a barrier between us and our target.

I push open the door, revealing a scene of opulence within. The room is adorned with luxurious furnishings, crystal chandeliers casting a soft glow over the space. The air is thick with the mingling scents of whiskey and anticipation.

Enzo sits at the center of a table, surrounded by his loyal men. His gaze flickers with a mix of arrogance and unease as he senses our presence. The tension in the room rises, the atmosphere crackling with the weight of impending confrontation.

Chaos erupts as the guests scatter, the room transforming into a battleground. The air fills with the sounds of gunfire and the shouts of men.

I move with precision, my instincts guiding me as I seek out Enzo among the chaos. Bullets whiz past me, narrowly missing their mark. The scent of gunpowder hangs in the air, mingling with the thick tension.

My gaze locks onto Enzo, his eyes filled with a mix of fear and defiance. His ducking out of my line of fire, behind his bodyguards.

"Enzo!" I call out, my voice cutting through the chaos. "It's over. There's nowhere left to hide."

I dash behind a table just as a bullet whizzes past my ears and then I yell out, "Enzo, come out you dumb fuck. You popped off at that dinner, but you thought I wouldn't come for you like this, didn't you?" My voice cutting through the room like a blade.

"Fuck off!" Enzo hollers out.

Guns start blaring again and I hear and see more bodies hit the floor. "Alright. Alright," Enzo screams and slides his guns out in the open. He emerges with his hands up in the air. I emerge out from behind a metal cain but I know my men have my back.

The tall lanky bastard smirks, his eyes glinting with defiance. "Dante, you've come to the wrong place at the wrong time."

My men spread out, taking strategic positions around the room. The tension is palpable, the silence stretching as we brace ourselves for the storm that is about to break.

I lock my gaze on Enzo as I shout, "Or maybe this is the right place at the right fucking time!" He smiles and steps back, his Italian leather shoes clicking against the hardwood floor.

"I'm not the one you want, Dante Argentieri," he says in a mocking tone. "I'm just a messenger."

My finger tenses on the trigger. "What the fuck do you mean?"

A sinister chuckle escaped from his lips. "Like I said...I'm just a messenger." In an instant, he ducks low and gracefully sidestepped away from me. A barrage of bullets shattered the silence as my guards engage with two men outside attempting to cover Enzo's escape.

I release a few rounds as well, aiming for one of their heads.

With lightning-fast reflexes, Enzo evades my shots and disappears into the crowd. I curse under my breath, frustration coursing through my veins. He's slipped through my fingers once again, leaving behind a trail of chaos and carnage.

Yet, in the midst of this turmoil, a fierce resolve burns within me. Enzo may have escaped for now and I've just learned that there's another player on the board.

The fire in my veins ignites, fueling my determination to protect and keep what's mine.

In the midst of the aftermath, there's one of Enzo's men left alive—one that didn't get away, but his life is ebbing away. His eyes meet mine, filled with a mixture of defiance and resignation. He knows he's lost, but he has a final message to deliver.

"Valeria Cipriano," he gasps, blood staining his lips. "Tell her... she's to report back... to the Cipriano Villa in Italy. She... she belongs... to the new boss now."

This is about her now. *They want her.*

Tired, cold, and bloody, I make my way back to the mansion and burst up the stairs to my bedroom. A storm of emotions is raging within me. I rip off the bloody clothes until I'm down to my boxers. I never liked wearing my enemy's or even my own blood—a reminder of what I've become and sometimes a reminder of defeat. I can't explain the anger that's racing through me right now. I want to end this now.

Valeria shuffles into the room. She's so quiet, always has been. That's why she'll always be a force to be reckoned with. If she were to ever lose her real innocence, no enemy will ever know she's coming. My father learned the hard way.

Her voice quivered as she said, "I heard you come in. I...I was waiting for you. Did something happen? Is everything okay?"

She doesn't see my bloody clothes. I've already put them away. I don't want to explain to her that I've killed again.

Her eyes search mine for answers. But I remain silent, my lips sealed, unwilling to reveal the dangerous path that lies ahead for her.

I reach my arm out for her to come inside. "Nothing I want you to be concerned about. I'm taking care of things. Need a shower. Just come to bed, Valeria."

"Okay," she whispers.

As she steps closer, her presence washes over me like a wave of calm. She hugs me. I wrap my arms around her, feeling her warmth enveloping me like a shield. She is my sanctuary—the bright light at the end of a tunnel and the rainbow after the storm. Her soft innocence is an offering of hope and comfort that I desperately need.

I need her. That's why I'm going to fight to keep her.

Thirty-Three

Dante

It's been almost a week since that fateful night at the casino, and the tension still hangs heavy in the air. I've been restless, my mind consumed with thoughts of what happened. The silence from their side is unnerving, and I know in my gut that this is far from over.

I haven't told Valeria about the message yet or that night. But things haven't changed. She knows that they want her —for what reason, we still don't know.

The Ciprianos weren't a threat before. Hell, even before my father and Valeria's father, Marco, agreed to an impasse, they weren't considered a low level threat to our existence. There had been no reason for me to keep tabs on the Ciprianos after Marco was murdered. His murder marked the downfall of that family—or so I thought. Furthermore, after Valeria shot my father, she became my entire family's public enemy number one. How could anyone have imagined that a fourteen year old girl would put down a revered mafia mob boss?

Now the Ciprianos want her back. I don't think that's all they want either. The Johnson embezzlement clearly tells me that.

I've taken every precaution to ensure Valeria's safety. She now has her own set of bodyguards, their watchful eyes never leaving her side. She's not allowed to step foot outside the property without them or me. It's a necessary measure, one that pains me to enforce after I promised her a some independence, but I won't take any chances with her life.

But a voice in my head keeps repeating that there are still some of my family members who think Valeria must pay for her role in my father's demise. Fortunately, they know better than to act on these thoughts, leaving me the sole authority to exact revenge if I choose to. Still, I know she doesn't deserve it.

The investigation into the Johnson embezzlement has led me down a twisted path. It seems Johnson unknowingly got involved with someone linked to Enzo and the Ciprianos. The pieces are falling into place, revealing an intricate web. I've delved deep into the underworld, gathering every bit of information I can, determined to unearth the truth.

Enzo could be hiding anywhere, biding his time, waiting for the perfect moment to strike again. He's cunning, resourceful, and I know underestimating him or their new boss would be a grave mistake. I can't let my guard down for even a moment, not when my empire and the woman I love are at stake. My father isn't here to guide me. He'd go in guns blazing. Shoot first. Ask questions later. That's his motto. I'm not sure that will get rid of the Ciprianos. After all, Valeria is a Cipriano. I don't want to rid myself of her.

Lost in my thoughts, I'm jolt back to reality by the sound of the door creaking open. Valeria strides into the room, her lips curved in a content smile. Water droplets glint off her tanned skin, illuminated by the sun's faint rays that enter through the windows. The white silk fabric of her coverup clings to her curves, and I can make out the pattern of her colorful bikini underneath. Her dark hair is wet and falls around her face in damp ringlets, and I can't help but lick my lips at the sight of her captivating beauty.

I quickly close my laptop and rise from my chair.

"Are you working on something important?" she asks, her eyes filled with curiosity and concern.

I reach out to her, pulling her close, and brush a tender kiss on her forehead. "Just taking care of some business," I reply, my voice laced with warmth. "But I'm glad you're here."

She strips off her coverup with carnal grace and saunters over to the window, the same windows I took her cherry up against. She then coyly lifts her arms above her head in a stretch and the way her pert ass cheeks peek out of that bikini bottom drives me wild. I know exactly why she's here—she comes to my office wearing nothing but the sexiest clothes just to remind me when it's time for me to put work aside and give her all of my attention. She has seen my dark side but she has chosen to shine her light upon me. I can almost feel her growing need and anticipation for my hard dick—which throbs harder by the second just looking at her.

I walk over to her by the window. She was silhouetted by the setting sun. I reached out and brushed my fingertips against the straps of her bikini top, feeling her sharp intake of breath as I tugged them down. Her breasts were soft in my hands, and I leaned forward to cup them, rolling my thumbs over her nipples so they puckered and hardened beneath me. Her body melted into mine as I bent to suckle on each one in turn, pushing her closer against me with every moan.

She peels away the bikini top, letting it drop to the ground and steps out of her bottoms. Her body is warm and inviting as she presses against me and I feel my heart racing in anticipation. My fingertips lightly brush over her smooth skin, tracing a path from her shoulders down to her wet pussy. She lets out a deep gasp of pleasure and throws her head back, inviting me closer with feral intensity. Our lips crash together in an explosive kiss that sends ripples of electrifying pleasure through our bodies.

Everything about her captivates me, and I ache for her with every fiber of my being. Gently I glide my hand up the velvety flesh of her body and linger on her curves, igniting a passionate fire within. I make my way to her chin as our lips part, but the desire that courses through me only intensifies with each passing second.

I couldn't help but admire the graceful curve of her neck as heat radiates from it. My fingertips lightly graze over her smooth skin, and I quickly wrap them around her neck in a possessive grip.

My name rolls off her lips in a languorous moan, and my body immediately responds, my dick becoming brick hard.

She drops to her knees without my asking because she knows exactly what I want.

I move her hair up and out of the way with my first and she wraps a small hand around my stiff dick. As soon as she touches me, precum leaks from the tip. She darts out her tongue to wet her lips and runs a single finger over the length of my pulsing erection. With gentle care, she guides me forward and wraps her full lips around me, her velvety tongue lapping up every inch I offered. She sucks me like she worships me and the way she looks up at me seductively through her dark long lashes nearly sends me over the edge. I face-fuck her until she's gagging on more than half of my dick. If I ram any further, I think she'll pass out. I want to fuck her pussy now because I know it's juicy wet.

I pull my dick out of her mouth and she releases me with an audible pop. I move behind her, grasping a fistful of her hair and tug it back until she's on her feet. Using my two fingers I motioned for her to follow me to the chair behind the desk and I sit down.

I stroke my dick up and down. "Sit on it."

She obeys, lifting one thigh over me until she's straddle me.

"Now give me that pretty fucking pussy," I whisper, desperate for her.

She sinks down my shaft until I'm fully enveloped in her tight little pussy. I thrust into her slick cunt, using my hands to pull her up and almost all the way off me and then I slam her back down on my dick.

"Dante..." Hearing the pleasure I give to her sends shivers through me. My veins heat up with desire and I pump like a jackhammer.

She comes first, throwing her head back in an ecstatic moment that's so beautiful I wish I could remember it forever. As she's panting, I grab her throat firmly and hammer into her with reckless abandon.

She reaches up and wraps her fingers around mine. I loosen my grip on her throat and she gasps for air.

"Never betray me," I hiss.

"Dante...I will...never betray you." She leans into me, rubbing her clit against my shaft. She knows how to use me to get off and I find that shit hot as fuck.

My tongue hungrily laps at her breasts, exploring every curve and crevice with a thirst that can never be quenched. Her nipples stand to attention as I lavish them with my love. Her skin seems to ignite beneath my touch as we lose ourselves in the heat of our passion. Every kiss and caress blazes with desperate intensity until our bodies feel like they're burning from inside out. Seconds later, my body erupts with the tremor of an orgasm, and she comes again too.

I'm still inside her slowly stroking upward in the aftermath. I want to fuck her again. I want to spend all night in this pussy. I want to spend eternity with her.

But our moment of tranquility is interrupted...

I hadn't heard them before, but the low humming of helicopter blades outside suddenly pierces through our safe haven, sending a chill down my spine. Without warning, bright lights blaze through the window followed by fiery sparks that spiral around outside like a shower of bullets. I am frozen in shock and that's not like me because no one on earth has ever *ever* brought chaos and destruction right to my home—aside from one person, but she's sitting on my dick.

The sound of heavy, determined footsteps marches towards the door like an approaching thunderstorm. Valeria and I hold our breaths in fear as the pounding grows closer. We stand up. I guard her with my body, grab my gun from under my desk, and turn towards the entrance.

My heart races as the figure approaches, and when they finally step through the doorway I feel like my entire world is crumbling down around me.

It's my father!

His eyes are ablaze with rage, and he's strapped with weapons that could turn this place into ashes if he wanted to. He looks like he's about to burn this whole motherfucker down.

Thirty-Four

Valeria

Leonardo Argentieri. It's him. The man I shot four years ago.

I can't be seeing a ghost. This looks real...but then it does not.

The world around me blurs into a frenzy of chaos and confusion as shattering our fragile sanctuary. I watch in horror as their confrontation escalates into a violent clash, their voices intertwining with rage and resentment. I'm frozen in place, my mind racing to comprehend the reality of this twisted situation.

"Why? Why weren't you there when I needed you the most?" Leonardo's voice booms with a mixture of anger and anguish. His eyes, once filled with paternal warmth, now glare at Dante with a burning fury.

"Father, you don't understand," Dante tries to defend himself, his voice strained. "I had no choice. I had to protect Valeria. I couldn't risk losing her."

"Protect her? From what? From me? From her own family? Because I've heard about what's going on, Dante." Leonardo's voice cracks with a deep sense of hurt. "I've spent months in a rehab facility, fighting to get back to you, and what do I find? You with the woman who shot me!"

I'm still trying to process what's going on. All this time. I thought he was dead.

"I spent years in a coma because of her." Leonardo pointed his gun at me spittle flying. "And then when I pulled out of it, you were too busy hunting her down and then fucking her, you failed to visit me. You would've known, son. But I'm a patient man..."

Tears well up in my eyes as the weight of Leonardo's pain and disappointment engulfs the room. My heart aches for the rift that has formed between father and son, for the choices that have led us to this moment.

"She's not like the others. She's not a threat to us." Dante pleads, his voice filled with desperation. "You know why she pulled that gun on you, Father."

Leonardo's eyes narrow, his face contorted with a mix of anger and sorrow. "Have you forgotten who we are? What we stand for? You're putting everything at risk, our family, our legacy, for this...this little whore. should've sent her straight to the brothel to be groomed like I planned all along. She's nothing more than a slut which is why you're fucking her in my office."

His words sting like a thousand knives, cutting through my already fragile emotions. The conflicting loyalties within me tug in opposite directions. I want to defend Dante, to tell Leonardo that he's wrong, that what we have is worth fighting for. But the truth lingers, casting a shadow over our bond. Can Dante truly protect me? Can he keep me safe from the darkness that surrounds us? His father hates me. He wants to kill me.

The room falls silent, the air thick with unspoken tension. Leonardo's gaze softens, his anger momentarily subdued, then he lunges and Dante meets him head on.

They were going at it, smashing and banging into everything in sight. It was a wild fight for who would come out on top. Father versus son. It shouldn't have come to this. My cries filled the room but nothing seemed to be able to break them apart. I was so scared, their rage echoing through me. Nothing could make them stop.

No one is coming and this night brings back memories of what happened years ago when I fled my own home in Italy.

Dante gains the upper hand, kicking away his father's weapon. He turns to me. "Run. The back."

Panic courses through my veins, but I do what he says.

"No, son, you don't get to do that. Not on my watch," Leonardo taunts his son behind me.

Before I reach the threshold, I hear a gunshot behind me. My body freezes, my instincts pulling me back to the source of danger. Another shot rings out and something like glass crashes to the floor.

My heart pounds as I whirl around and catch a glimpse of Dante. Blood trickles from his side, dripping onto the carpet beneath his feet and staining it a deep crimson. My hands clench involuntarily as he staggers out of the office, hunched over in pain, his face gaunt with suffering. Tears stream down my cheeks as I watch him try to stop the bleeding with shaking hands.

Confusion floods my mind as our eyes meet, and I falter, trying to comprehend the gravity of the situation. "You have to go," he croaks, his voice laced with desperation and pain.

"But... your father," I stammer, struggling to find the words, my heart torn between loyalty and a yearning to understand.

"You put him in a coma," Dante confesses, his voice strained. "He was on an island. Only a few know the secret. We were...we were trying to buy him time to reclaim his place. I didn't... I didn't know he was awake. No one knew if he'd ever wake."

The realization crashes over me like a tidal wave, drowning me in a sea of guilt and confusion. And now, the consequences of our entangled fate unfold before me.

"Did you...shoot him?" I look behind as we descend the stairs.

"Yes, but I know he isn't dead... he never dies," Dante murmurs, his words carrying a weight I cannot fully comprehend.

I search his eyes, desperately trying to make sense of what he said. His fingers softly brush the strands of my hair away from my face, and I feel a warmth flush through me as his lips graze mine for a single moment. "I don't disappear, Valeria. I don't run," he says, firmly.

My chest tightens as I feel the first stirrings of fear, my quivering legs barely keeping me upright.

"Be ready when I come for you because I will come," he says.

Suddenly, his heavy hand was on my shoulder and he pushes me forcefully into the waiting car. The door slams closed before I can react, and the engine roars to life.

"Dante," I scream out his name in desperation, my voice echoing throughout the backseat. There's only me, a driver, and a passenger. "Come with me! *Dante.*" I bang on the windows and try to open the door, but nothing gives.

I press my trembling hands against the window, my eyes locked on Dante's diminishing figure, his torment etched across his face.

PART 2 ~ UNTIL IT ENDS ~ COMING SOON

DON'T MISS THE NEXT BOOK LAUNCH!
For Jada's new release news, copy, paste, & subscribe --> CLICK HERE.

An Invitation

DON'T MISS THE NEXT BOOK LAUNCH!
For Jada's new release news, copy, paste, & subscribe -->
CLICK HERE.

About the Author

Jada Dark is an emerging author of dark, gritty, and spicy contemporary romance.

Printed in Great Britain
by Amazon